CIRSOVA PRESENTS™:

Michael Tierney's

WILD STARS® V:

THE ARTOMIQUE PARADIGM

Written by Michael Tierney

Edited by Xavier L and Mark Thompson

Cover Art by Cover Art by Anton Oxenuk and Genzoman

Illustrations by DarkFilly and Michael Tierney

Layout & Design by P. Alexander

WILD STARS V:

THE ARTOMIQUE PARADIGM

Prelude:
Orcas in the Caribbean
International Waters
2005

"Blackfish," said Kearston, pointing to a trio of tall, dark, triangular fins that repeatedly broke the water's surface.

"That's maybe only the fourth pod of orcas ever sighted in the Caribbean," Carlton MacKanaly replied. "And I do mean ever...in recorded history."

"Counting yesterday?" Finding him to be quite handsome, with his rugged physique from the constant physical activity of life as a divemaster, Kearston tried to establish a familiarity for later, when she would have to kill him. She pushed his mind only slightly with her telepathy, sensing the kindred soul of a survivor left alone and adrift in life.

"No, it's got to be the same pod." He finished attaching a buoyancy control vest and scuba regulator assembly to an air tank and opened the valve. The vest and hoses all stiffened with pressure at the same time. Taking a test breath out of both second stage regulators, Carlton added, "It's unusual to see them loitering in one area."

"Think they'll give us any trouble?" Kearston raised her arms and retied the strap of her one-piece swimsuit behind her neck, but he never seemed to notice as she flaunted herself. His mind was on another woman he considered to be unattainable.

"Doubt it, they're not interested us." He began gearing up a second air tank, glancing distractedly out across the waves, as if searching for a danger he could sense but not quite place. "But *something* attracted them to this area. It's fine with me if you want to sit out the dive. I've got this."

Kearston shook her head. "I'm here for a job. Just like you."

She noticed how two figures watched her from behind the glass of the wheelhouse. It seemed that all Earthmen had the gift of telepathy on some level. Just as Carlton sensed trouble, the men who wanted him dead worried whenever she talked with him. Trying to hide things from her was foolish of them and caused her misgivings.

"Glad you know what that job is," said Carlton, "because I'm not sure why you're here."

"I've already told you," she scanned the blue, sun-kissed Caribbean waters that surrounded them on all sides, with no land anywhere in sight, "and you can't beat the working conditions."

"Priority oversight of industrial secrets. Right... just don't get too relaxed while you're making sure I don't hook a cable up in the wrong spot."

"I'll be careful. I know you've had some tense dives in the past."

"Yeah." He looked up when a deck hatchway opened and a man wearing a light blue polo shirt and khaki shorts climbed up from below. "But not as bad as some people."

She patted the newcomer on the shoulder as she passed him on her way the stairs leading to the wheelhouse.

"I could hear you two talking," Genghis Champlain said as she closed the wheelhouse door behind her.

"He's a brave man." Kearston looked down at the two men talking in the assembly area, but her attention was focused on gently probing Genghis's subconscious.

"Carlton MacKanaly?" Genghis clearly did not like to hear anything close to a compliment being said about him.

"No. Well, yes, him too. But I was talking about Rich Stanton. He's overwhelmed by fear of being eaten alive by a shark every time he looks at the water. He's being very brave, trying to hide that fear from us."

"It's necessary," said Genghis. "He was our hook to lure MacKanaly here."

That was when she caught a memory of Genghis sitting in a helicopter with three other men, one of whom she had never met. The stranger had a lantern jaw and piercing blue eyes that were shadowed beneath heavy eyebrows. Even the normally unflappable Genghis was intimidated to his core by his memory of this man, who firmly declared how he not only wanted MacKanaly dead, he wanted every memory of him ever being alive to be erased. It seemed like a flight of fantasy, but she could tell that Genghis considered it his job to make this stranger's every request happen. Then she caught a hint of something deeper and far scarier.

"You knew Mack wouldn't turn down a job from a man saved," she probed deeper. "Still, Stanton coming back to the area where he watched his wife eaten alive by a tiger shark," she shivered, "he can't stop thinking about it. And he puts that horror in my head every time I'm around him."

"So that's why you always avoid him? Just stop reading his mind."

She found it ironic coming from him at the very moment when she was probing *his* mind. She had already known that Genghis and his fellow Artomiques were somehow allied with the alien Brothan. She had been sent to make contact with them to investigate their alliance. But until this very moment, she did not realize how deep their connection went with the formidable wolf-like aliens.

"It's not that simple," she replied.

"Well, Kearston, do what you have to do. Once MacKanaly does the job, he's a dead man—even if it is a few years late. After that, Stanton is expendable, too."

"Do you have to kill them both?" She feigned slight disinterest, while her own mind reeled from having seen Genghis's memory of an apocalyptic destruction of his Earth, where the very fabric of his reality had been rent asunder and replaced by the world currently around them. She looked away to hide any reaction her face might reveal.

"No." Genghis gave the back of her head a hard look, as she tried not to react to the realization of how long and hard the Artomiques had schemed to recreate their own world. Only recently had they begun to accept the possibility that this might never happen. "That depends on you."

Having collected herself from the initial shock of what she had uncovered, Kearston turned back to face Genghis. His darker skin and face reflected his direct descent from his namesake, Genghis Khan, while his blue eyes came from an Artomique father— German in this reality.

She could see herself reflected in those eyes and could hear his mind trying to decipher her own genetic mix, which defied Earth-bound perceptions. With slightly tan skin and light brown hair that framed high cheekbones and green eyes, only a handful of people on Earth would recognize her as a child of the Wild Stars—distant planets that few on Earth realized existed. Now that the Wild Stars had vanished from the galaxy, they might never know.

"If you want to find your way back into the stars"—Genghis seemed to read her mind, though she knew that was not possible—"then you need to help us recover that spaceship."

"It's a Wild Stars ship?" she asked.

"Not just any ship. Our recent takeover of the collapsed Granite Rock Bank provided us with intel that indicates this a scout class Wild Stars ship, which is..."

"The fastest ship in the galaxy," she interjected before he could say it. She finally understood what it was Genghis was hiding. He and the other Artomiques were not just using this salvage dive as an excuse to kill a hated enemy, whom, for some strange reason unclear to her, they blamed for the destruction of their world. No, what they were really hiding was how their plans had shifted to increasing their influence and control over the reality where they found themselves stranded. They had plans to assert their Artomique Paradigm on the world, regardless of however long that effort might take.

"Not just that. We believe that this ship was lost by Erlik, son of the Ancient Warrior."

She blinked, a visual break in her struggle to control her outward reactions and not reveal the impact of his words. That she was a member of the secret organization of female telepaths known as the Five Thousand Fingered Hand, the Artomiques were already aware. What she could not allow them to learn was how it was manipulations by the Hand that most likely caused the Ancient Warrior to relocate the Wild Stars to parts unknown. Their plans to manipulate the Wild Stars had backfired in spectacular fashion.

"That ship not only has an artificial intelligence operating system," Genghis continued, "it has a supply of exotic matter. According to our information, Erlik overloaded the ship's systems while teleporting something big off-world and had to abandon the ship. There is also a chance that some autonoman might be on board."

"Auto-what?" She feigned ignorance.

"Autonoman. Synthetic men with weapons and flight systems built into their bodies, controlled by an autonomous A.I. operating system. Erlik was known to use them as bodyguards on occasion. The technology on that ship could power the Artomique Corporation to the cutting edge of new technologies for hundreds of years."

"So, which is it you want? The ship? Or Carlton MacKanaly dead?"

"Both. Achilles Hister vowed that MacKanaly must die. But get the ship secured on the lifting cables before you give him a brain aneurysm or whatever it is you plan to cause him to drown. Leave the body down there—lost at sea. Once he leaves this deck, I never want to see his face again."

The waters were so warm, neither Kearston nor Carlton wore a wetsuit. They geared up and took turns stepping through the gate in the railing and dropping into the sea. She had used her mind-reading skills to answer his every question when Carlton had grilled her in advance, concerned by the fact that she had no certification card to assure him of her abilities. He seemed to suspect that this was her very first open water dive, even as she locked in on his subconscious and mimicked his every action and reflex.

She checked her gear just as he did, then purged the excess air from her buoyancy control vest and followed him down the rope attached to the marker buoy he had previously set. When he put a hand on the cables dropping next to them, she did the same.

Suddenly, Kearston felt a wave of apprehension and claustrophobia, but quickly realized that it came from Carlton. A deeply rooted memory had revealed itself. He had once been chained to a bucket of concrete and thrown into a deep river to drown, yet managed to walk his way back to the surface—how, he never understood. He fought off the wave of panic, and his entire thought patterns changed.

Kearston marveled at how quickly all his uneasiness vanished. Here, he was in his element. He understood the dangers of this undersea world well. Still, it seemed strange to Kearston that a man who had nearly died by drowning would choose a profession where he made his living underwater.

Then she understood.

He was facing his fears.

From that point on, she was enthralled by the canopy of aquatic life and colorful corals sixty feet down, which spread abundantly across the ocean floor. At the end of the rope was something decidedly out of place—a gleaming gold starship, although she could read the confusion about what it was in Carlton's mind.

He had examined the ship thoroughly when he had first discovered it and had no idea what it truly was. His best guess was that it must be a prototype submersible.

Carlton quickly set to work securing the cables according to a plan formulated after his initial dive. A large loop was hooked around the object's conical nose and smaller loops around the wing-like structures on the upper rear. Once he secured the last cable that linked the others into place, he looked back to confirm with Kearston that there were no problems.

This was the moment she had been recruited for.

It was time for Carlton MacKanaly to die.

Even through his mask, she could see a look of

concern in his eyes, which she attributed to his innate telepathic ability. But then she realized that he was looking past her and saw the danger reflected in both his mind and face-mask at the same time. Something green, nightmarish, and possibly humanoid had risen from the depths directly behind her, and she had never sensed a thing. As frightening as the thought was that any living creature could catch her unawares, what she turned to see right on top of her was even more startling.

Long, webbed fingers with curved claws clamped over her facemask as the powerful creature whisked her away. Blinded, she reached out and made an even deeper telepathic connection with Carlton's mind, seeing what he saw.

Carlton did not waste a moment considering the impossibility of the strange creature that seized Kearston. He instinctively did what he always did in dire situations—he acted to intercede.

Several more fishmen shot out of the shadows lining the sea bottom. But they weren't attacking him. Instead, they carried what looked like bizarrely complex bolt cutters as they headed for the rising ship. But before they could reach their goal, a trio of dark forms appeared out of the deep blue like underwater freight trains. Each member of the pod of orcas seized a fishman in its jaws and disappeared as quickly as it had appeared.

The fishman carrying Kearston was un-deterred by the calamity that had befallen his fellows, and continued to carry her down into a black grotto.

Kearston caught a glimpse of Carlton's hand slipping into the wrist-hoop connected to his flashlight before he unclipped it from his vest. Following her captor into the grotto, his tiny beam of light became fainter and fainter as the distance between them became ever greater, and she slowly lost telepathic contact.

She began to feel giddy, losing her fright, and realized that they must have already descended well below a hundred feet—possibly two. One of the last thoughts she intercepted from Carlton was a concern over nitrogen narcosis, which some divers referred to as being *narked* because of the drunken feeling caused by the buildup of nitrogen bubbles in the blood.

Despite being trapped in darkness, she became so relaxed that she passed out.

"Wake up!" Kearston felt a pair of steel-strong hands shaking her shoulders and opened her eyes to see Carlton MacKanaly standing over her in the semi-darkness of a cave, only slightly illuminated by his nearby flashlight.

"What happened?"

"That thing that took you left you in this underwater cave with an air pocket. It was gone by the time I caught up with you."

Carlton picked up his light and shined it around.

"I don't think this is a cave," Kearston echoed his thoughts.

They found themselves next to a pool at the center of a marble-walled room, filled with cracked pillars that still supported a stone roof high overhead. Pieces of fallen masonry littered the floors, and ornate statues of gold-adorned marble stood everywhere—all of them facing the pool.

"This is an ancient temple." Carlton focused his light on the colossal carving of a man wearing a crown, whose lower body was that of a fish.

"Dagon," said Kearston. "Three thousand years ago, Philistines worshipped this god of the sea, among many others. But his was only one of many religions that they absorbed during their prior history as Aegean seafarers. Worship of Dagon dates further back that any recorded history. There are some isolated communities that still hold the sea-lord in reverence."

"Fish-gods?" Carlton asked incredulously. "We're a long way from the Aegean."

"I think we just met some of Dagon's descendants, and it looks like they're back."

Other lights began to appear around them as figures emerged from recently cut tunnels in the walls. Those carrying light-sticks at the forefront were more of the agile fishmen they had encountered earlier, while those following behind them looked more like lobster-men, with thick carapaces on their backs and long metal spears in their webbed hands.

One of the lobster-men stepped to the front. This one looked different, with strange eye-stalks growing out of its head. The orbs fixated on Kearston and Carlton.

A webbed finger pointed at Kearston.

"You are like me," she heard the thought in her head.

The creature then motioned for the others to surround her and Carlton, using their spears to usher them in the direction of one of the tunnels. There they saw what looked like a crude, metal cart, mounted on a rail that led downward.

"What weren't you telling me about that thing we were lifting?" Carlton looked around, measuring his chances in a fight. "Does it belong to them?"

"Absolutely not," she replied. "I have no idea why these creatures attacked us. But I may know what they are."

"This should be interesting."

"Have you ever heard of the Wild Stars?"

"Wasn't that a comic book series?"

"Huh? I have no idea what you're talking about. The Wild Stars are the region of space where mankind colonized when they made their first migration off-world."

"Huh?"

"They were nearly chased forever from the Earth by the sea creatures known as the Isshla. It's from them that the term *island* comes, but the Isshla claim all land surrounded by the seas."

"When it comes down to it, you're talking about the whole planet."

"Basically. They would have taken complete control, but the man called the Ancient Warrior, who guided the way to the Wild Stars, returned and found a way to defeat the Isshla. Somehow he imprisoned them deep inside the Earth."

"Okay." Carlton abandoned his plan for hopeless resistance and put his hands up as he and Kearston were prodded to enter the metal cart.

"You don't believe me?"

"Nope. I think you know more about comic books than you're letting on. And I doubt that it's a coincidence that they showed up at that salvage ship."

The cart started rolling them away into the darkness and quickly picked up speed, and they descended ever deeper into the bowels of the Earth. She felt a queasiness in the pit of her stomach and read Carlton's mind about swallowing hard to release the pressure building on her ears, even while he continued to belabor his point.

"What *is* inside that thing?"

Chapter One:
Battle by the Nebula

"As you know, all of our Artomique technology is based on the recovery of a single Wild Stars ship," said Genghis Champlain. "In a galaxy rife with strife, but struggling for peace, we are humanity's only true hope. We can't let our past be revealed and have all of our plans become undone. Not now... not when we're so close to initiating our ultimate gambit."

Achilles 'Whip' Hister knew that Genghis was pandering to him, but why—he was not sure. Neither did Whip know what this ultimate plan was that had always been kept a secret from him. He bit his tongue and bided his time while examining the long-range satellite image of a colorful nebula cloud that his mentor had overlaid onto the wall that served as the main portal for the observation lounge. Soon, Whip would become arguably the most powerful man alive. All he had to do was be patient a little longer.

"I refuse to believe it's a coincidence that the ion trail of the escaped Saturnian-Eybontic hybrid is headed in the same direction as where our satellite links have shown a facial recognition hit from our blacklist."

As he talked, Genghis kept a hand cupped over his ear, receiving constant updates from the captain on the ship's bridge. Their ship, Godspeed, was fresh off the production line and on its maiden voyage, which, by the numbers, was the most dangerous flight by any starship. But those numbers continued to improve as Earth became both better astral navigators and shipbuilders, and their dreadnought redefined what it meant to be a top of the line vessel.

Whip dialed up a holographic projection that manifested directly in front of the screen and magnified an area in intricate detail that revealed the remains of what had once been a Marzanti Worldship—an alien vessel so large that it could not enter a solar system without disrupting the rotation of the planets. Centering and enlarging the focus revealed three figures fighting amid the wreckage.

"That's him, all right." Georgian Raveling entered the lounge the moment after Whip enlarged the image enough to show facial features. "Bully Shawnee triggered the recognition signal. He's also called Stormbringer, Zarawtic, and a lot of other things. He's the grandson of Mark MacKavicka, nicknamed Mack, Codenamed: First Marker. Mack has repeatedly escaped our assassins. Defying death seems to be a hereditary trait that Shawnee inherited."

"Weren't the events in the First Marker file... like two hundred years ago?" Whip asked. "How old can his grandson be?"

"Mack popped up again during the Cybernetics War." Genghis began rotating surveillance images across a section of the lounge screen. "Then again a little over twenty years ago, when he was active on Akara's World. More recently, he's been sighted on several of the newly returned Wild Stars worlds, including Ansa. And I agree with you, it looks like he hasn't aged much for all that time."

"Hasn't aged... much?" Whip admonished the comment, pretending not to notice how Genghis was systematically deactivating the red grids that kept popping along on the corners of the portal. "He hasn't aged at all! Still, with all the enhancements and training that you've had since your ancestor encountered him, I'd say this time a Champlain would beat him in a fight."

"I'm ready."

"And the Champlain who lost that fight," said Georgian, "has already had a revenge—of sorts."

There was something about the certainty with which Genghis replied that Whip found odd. Both of the regents Whip's father had left to manage the Artomique Corporation until his coming of age had always displayed an uncanny familiarity whenever discussing their ancestors. It was a familiarity filled with knowledge nowhere to be found in the archives.

"That man holds not only the secret to altering reality, he can move through time," Georgian asserted.

When Genghis gave no further reply other than the nod of his head, Whip motioned for him to speak.

"The captain says that they still can't recover the Eybontic's signal. If he stalls the engines any more, we'll drop out of hyper-light drive. He suggests that we resume course for Ansa."

"Tell him to drop out of light drive," Whip replied. "We're not done here."

"We can't afford the delay," Georgian argued. "Do you want to be late for your Terraformer rendezvous? Maybe miss your own celebration? Your father has planned this for a long time. When you come of age, not only do you become the head of Artomique Corp, you'll become the most powerful man in the galaxy. That's something more than a few people might want to stop from happening. This could be a trap."

Whip repeated his order.

Genghis exchanged a look with Georgian before relaying Whip's message, but as the view outside the window turned from milky white into a colorful star panorama, he relayed another warning.

"The captain wants me to remind you how dangerous this sector of space is," said Genghis. "There's an entire squadron of Equine Class warships assisting a Maxitrillion Class warship that is in hot pursuit of the extra-dimensional Neth entity. All of that is happening inside the Nebula we're looking at."

"I know." Whip waved his hand in the direction of the massive debris field—when the Nebula behind it was lit up from within by staccato flashes of colorful light. "That's the remains of the Marzanti world-ship that the wormhole monster Neth appropriated. That Maxitrillion warship blasted it into pieces."

"Now they've pursued the entity deep inside that nebula," said Georgian. "Being a gaseous entity, it's going to be in its own element there. And, since its mate, Nean, was destroyed, it's going to be angry, too."

As if to emphasize Genghis's point, the core of the nebula flashed an immense wave of light. Either a star had gone supernova, or the battle was intensifying to horrific levels. All the local images that they were watching flashed as the source shifted from a nearby satellite to the Godsend's optics—with the ship's unique side-to-side motion in space-normal speed providing a constantly shifting perspective on the holographic display.

"Tell the captain to scan that nebula and pick up any readings on that Maxitrillion ship that our competitors built. While he's at it, scan that debris field. We need to learn anything we can about Marzanti technology."

"Yes, sir," Genghis replied with the same obedience his ancestors had shown for two hundred years—ever since they had crossed over from an alternate reality world where fascism had conquered the world in the name of the Artomiques. They had always named their most deadly warships in honor of that lost heritage. "But the captain again wants me to remind…"

"Yes, yes," said Whip. "It's dangerous out here. I know. That's why we're in the newest Artomique class dreadnought. Tell him that I know we'll be late for my meeting with the Terraformer heiress, but this is an opportunity we can't pass up."

"Sir," said Genghis. "They've relocated the signal. They've found the hybrid Dalucar again!"

"Where?"

"There!" Genghis pointed to Whip's hologram of three men fighting in the debris field. "The reason they lost his signal is the hybrid stopped on that big chunk of the ship that's shaped like an enormous face. He's one of those combatants. I knew this couldn't be a coincidence."

"Reports said that section was reshaped by Neth into his own image," said Whip. "What is Dalucar doing?" He tapped the window to activate another holographic control panel and zoomed in. "We know who one of the people he's fighting is, but who's that other man? Why didn't the recognition software pick up either him or Dalucar?"

"The Eybontics were destroyed," Georgian replied, "except for the last one that Earth-gov locked away in their Gates of Hell. And all the Saturnians were exiled on chunks of ice from Oort

Cloud and sent flying. Neither the Eybontics nor the Saturnians were ever programmed into the system."

The enlarged image revealed the sentient machine-man battling with two bubble-helmeted men who wielded what were either photonic-laser blades or turquoise-colored swords. Then Whip realized that the blades were curved, which photonic blades could never be.

The machine-man known as an Eybontic was a sentient entity whose entire humanoid form was filled with lethal weapons and a personal propulsion system that enabled it to achieve light speeds. Why it would have chosen to stop and engage in a fight was a mystery. What was even more surprising was the way that the Eybontic was unable to overwhelm his opponents. Somehow, the bubble-helmeted men were always able to either deflect the Eybontic's attacks with their blades, which should not have been possible, or literally disappeared and reappeared to renew the attack from an unexpected vector.

"Who can that other man be?" Genghis queried.

"No way to know," Georgian replied. "But we're going to find out. Do recognition searches from these recordings."

"Nothing about him is registering," said Genghis. "His face isn't in any known database."

"Strange to think that the body of the last of the Eybontics would be inhabited by Dalucar," said Whip, "the last known Saturnian. They were mortal enemies. It was a stroke of luck when Dalucar somehow broke that Eybontic out of that Venusian prison. All my life I've worried that someone would figure out that one of Georgian's ancestors designed the Eybontics as autonomous deep-space explorers before they gained sentience."

"And since the Saturnians gained their long lives from our cloning technology," said Genghis, "the Artomique Corporation created both sides of a conflict that killed fifteen billion people. If anyone on Earth ever figured that out, the reputation of Artomique Corp would never recover. Even today, generations later, we'd be hated war criminals."

"Not anymore," said Whip. "Now that the Wild Stars have returned, we can blame them. Before, no one would have believed we stole those technologies from a Wild Stars ship recovered from the bottom of the Gulf of Mexico. Now... now they might. People are finally starting to realize that the Wild Stars are real and not a myth. Look! The fight's over!"

Inexplicably, two men armed with simple swords had defeated a machine-man who supposedly could not be defeated by mere men. They had sliced him into pieces that scattered in the weightlessness of the void.

"What the...?" Genghis muttered when the other man handed his sword to Bully Shawnee and simply disappeared. Then Shawnee vanished. "When did he gain that skill?"

"It might explain why members of his family don't age," Whip hypothesized.

"We've heard about men like that," said Georgian. "That other man must be Purple Order, from the galaxy of the deathless entity the Wild Starriors call the God Father."

"Tell the captain to move in and recover whatever remains he can," said Whip.

"Why bother with the recognition search?" asked Genghis. "If that third man is from another galaxy, it will be a waste..."

"Do it anyway," said Whip. "If someone from this galaxy has figured out how to incorporate the abilities of the Purple Order, I want that knowledge. Once we get what we want, we'll do with it what we always do."

Whip said the words that were expected of him but did not feel the conviction. His entire life had been spent in isolation and training to take over his father's role as Cheif Executive and Chief Operating Officer. When Achilles Hister the 7th departed to explore the Wild Stars, he had left Whip in charge of the Corporation, with guidance from his regents.

Whip highlighted a section of the wall grid, where the Eybontic's head floated, its glowing eyes slowly growing dim.

"Tell the captain to send a service drone to recover that," he ordered Genghis, who hesitated at first, but a nod and a shrug from Georgian seemed to tip his judgement.

Now Whip did what he had always done during his long periods of isolation—and threw himself into the quest for discovery.

Once the recovered head of the Eybontic was delivered to him and the ship had returned on course for Ansa, he locked himself away in the main science laboratory and activated a faraday cage program to secure the room from the rest of the ship.

Before he powered the Eybontic's brain back up, Whip went through and deleted all the programming with the largest personality profiles, figuring that would eradicate the entity called Dalucar. He then picked out a profile that looked incomplete, which was unusual since Saturnians were knowledge vampires who normally sucked the whole essence out of a victim's brain. Whip made that personality into the operating system interface.

Once hooked into an energy outlet, the disembodied head began to rattle and shake. Then the eyes lit up.

"Here I go again," the voice box spoke without movement of the mouth. "Still a severed head. This is a new one, but just like before, I still have no sensory input."

"Who are you?" Whip asked.

"Carthage," the head replied, "of the Wild Stars."

"When did Dalucar Zonderman victimize you?"

"Long before... and long after I was injected with the Bioenergetic formula..."

Whip was instantly enthralled. He had read about the supposedly mythical formula from ancient World War Two documents that were still considered classified. He had no idea that anyone had ever actually synthesized the biological weapon that turned men into zombies.

"President Bully Bravo had my undead head imprisoned with the severed head of the Saturnian, Dalucar. Either he was showing mercy by giving us each someone to talk to, or he was cruelly punishing us. I don't know which. Bravo ordered all electronics to be removed from our prison, as part of the old Saturnian Protocols from the war. When newly elected President Perez allowed electronics back, Dalucar escaped within hours, taking part of me with him as a last gesture of spite."

"Which part of your consciousness is still back

with your undead head?"

"Considering how I'm not angry anymore, I'd say it was the part filled with hate. It was the only thing I could feel after becoming one of the undead. Don't know why I felt that way, since all the bad things that ever happened to me, I brought on myself."

"Just how did you... Dalucar... escape?" Whip asked.

"Knowledge," the head replied. "I thought he was constantly rattling at me to drive me insane, but he was piquing the interest of the guards. Finally, something he said got the new President's attention."

"What was that?"

"The location of Asgard. Sorry, that's what New Atlantis was called in the Norse legends. Dalucar told them he knew where the capitol planet of the Wild Stars was hidden."

"I thought their capitol was Ansa?"

"No," the head replied. "That's where the Ancient Warrior's son, Erlik, holds court. But the real power of the Wild Stars lies on the world called New Atlantis, rotating around the galactic plate in a secret position. President Perez wanted that location, sent a recorder, and snap... Dalucar was gone and took me with him."

"Tell me, did you know where Dalucar was going? Why was he headed in the direction of Ansa?"

"He wanted revenge on the man who imprisoned him. That's why he stopped to fight. He wants to hurt that man every way he can."

"The same man who imprisoned you?"

"Former President Bully Bravo."

"I know who the blond man that you... or rather, Dalucar... was fighting. Do you know who the other man is?"

"He's President Bravo's son," Carthage replied.

"Bully Bravo had no children."

"Dalucar was headed straight for Bully Bravo. His only plan was for revenge. He wouldn't have detoured for anything, except the opportunity to kill the president's illegitimate son, Bullson."

Whip was stunned by what he had heard.

"How much do Bully Shawnee and Bullson know about the origin of the Eybontics and Saturnians?" he asked.

"Like I once was, they're both time travelers, so there is a high probability that they know about many of the things that your Artomique Corporation has done."

"Like what?"

"How you created both the Saturnians and the Eybontics and caused the Cybernetics War. And even if they don't know, once the now-returned Wild Stars learn about what happened, they will recognize that their own technology has been misused. Also..."

Whip disconnected the power and dimmed the lights. He sat there for a long moment, watching to see if there was any activity from the artificial head, worrying that some element of the Saturnian might have found a way to reassert itself and make a cybernetic escape. He ran a diagnostic of all the laboratory's operating systems and breathed a sigh of relief when it revealed no abnormal activity.

He then encased the Eybontic head in a cabinet made from non-conductive materials, which no electronic signal could penetrate. For the briefest of moments, he imagined the red eyes of the skull reactivating with energy inside the safe's inky darkness, and he felt pity for the remnants of the man once called Carthage—sealed in a cybernetic cage with his tormentor. Then Whip remembered who he was and how he had no time for such petty distractions.

Between the threat of old secrets being revealed and the new secrets that his own mentors were keeping from him, a nagging intuition that something terrible was about to happen began to overwhelm Whip. He sat and stared at a remote image of the approaching Wild Stars moon, Ansa, as it circled the gas giant, Behemit. It seemed to him that the filaments of gas clouds from the Dragon's Claw Nebula in the background were indeed forming talons that reached out to ensnare him... or shake his hand.

Whip had made his own secret plans to reshape the Artomique Corporation in ways that his mentors never suspected, nor would approve.

He only had to wait a little bit longer.

Chapter Two:
Highways in the Sky

"Look at him," the woman sneered as former United States President Bully Bravo greeted new arrivals to Ansa at an adjacent gateway. "I can't stand the sight of him."

"Is that Bully Bravo?" asked Whip as he stepped through. He had never seen the former President in person. Bravo had a barrel chest, a military haircut, and a regimented demeanor that no amount of time away from the services could diminish. But his legendary grim visage had softened after he learned to smile during his career as a politician.

"Yes, sorry." She extended a hand in greeting as her two burly bodyguards eyed Genghis and Georgian. "I'm Josette Mcguffin, heiress to the Terraformer Corporation. Welcome to Ansa, young Mister Hister."

"Whip," he replied to the evident chagrin of his regents.

"I believe this is your first visit to the stars?"

"It's my first visit anywhere," Whip cut his eyes at his overprotective guardians. "When I take over the C.E.O's seat, it's going to be a new dawn for the Artomique Corporation. I'm on a goodwill mission in preparation for that day."

"Well," Josette replied, "my ship takes off in a little while. I was beginning to think you wouldn't make it for our meeting before I left."

"Sorry, we were delayed. Are you planning to

return for the Earth-Wild Stars conference?"

"No. The Terraformers have never been properly acknowledged for all we've done to colonize the stars. Until we are, I want no part of their treaty discussions. When they're ready to terraform new worlds, it will be on my terms, not theirs."

"I'm ready to discuss terms, now." Whip was slightly distracted by the lightness of his step with Ansa's lighter gravity.

"At least, we're ready to open a dialog," Genghis interjected.

"Come," she led the way to a nearby door, where two men in plain clothes passed them through. "Let's relax in the executive lounge and discuss things further. You've got one-half of an Earth hour before I have to leave."

"Why the rush?" Whip took a seat, while his mentors hovered as near as Mcguffin's bodyguards were willing to permit.

"Pirate activity. They're not too keen to see this conference lead to new treaties. If you just came from Earth, I'm surprised you didn't have an encounter with them yourself. It's just going to get even worse after the conference, I'm afraid."

"I hadn't heard about any trouble from pirates." Whip tried to make eye contact first with Genghis and then Georgian, hoping to check their reactions, but both men looked away. "I thought all that trouble ended when the Whisper Ice Cream heiress, Scarlet Tanager, disappeared."

"After it was revealed that she was the Red Queen, Nefarimor, everyone said she was dead," said Josette. "Rumor has it that she was eaten by red grief on Akara's World."

"That doesn't make any sense," said Whip. "Everyone abandoned that cursed world after it was infested by the Brothan."

"Thing about rumors is they can be complete fiction. There has been a new rumor that Nefarimor never left Corsairiana."

"Regardless of treaties or pirates," said Whip with conviction, "I believe the Terraformers and the Artomiques will do considerable business in the future. We build the biggest ships, and we're going to need bases for our transit networks. Earth and the Wild Stars might be shaking hands, but their ideologies are not compatible. While they're discovering that, you and I will build the highways in the sky."

Josette twirled a curl of dark hair in her index finger, emptied her drink, and stood up.

"I almost didn't agree to this meeting. Your father has a reputation of being a little... abrasive. But I believe you and I can work together."

They walked together toward the exit, discussing terms for laying down a groundwork for negotiations, mostly to be conducted by Georgian Raveling. Josette seemed a little put off by that suggestion at first, but then she saw Bully Bravo waiting for them outside in the main aisle.

"Let's make it happen," she said as she quickly walked away, returning Bully Bravo's greeting with a cold nod of her head, her eyes turned.

Bully then greeted Whip and his companions.

"It's a pleasure to meet you, Mister President," Whip lied. "Something I can do for you?"

"Very perceptive of you," Bully smiled. "Yes, I have been waiting. While I'm no longer a representative of Earth's government, people make inquiries of me all the time. Many of those inquiries have been about when your new line of dreadnoughts will be available to assist with Earth's evacuation."

"I'd heard that the Wild Stars already dealt with crisis of the runaway black hole, Ruin," said Whip.

Bully nodded.

"Ruin is no longer headed for the center of the solar system," he conceded. "But, like a line of dominoes, when you push one—others start falling."

Whip looked at Georgian when the President used his counselor's own analogy.

"Ruin was knocked out of its symbiotic orbit with Earth," said Bravo. "Now that it's been removed completely, something like it needs to take its place in the celestial clockwork. There is a chance that assistance from our allies in the Wild Stars might be able to correct the situation. But until that happens, we should continue the evacuation."

Genghis decided to insert himself into the conversation.

"You're counting on help from a race of people,"

he said, "whose wars are what put Earth in danger?"

"You seem to know a lot of details about Ruin that most don't," said Bravo. "I was there when it was thrown out of the galaxy. These people from the Wild Stars can do things, teach us things that you would not believe. I'm glad that you've accepted my invitation to this conference. I hope we can make a treaty between Earth, the Wild Stars, and all Earth's colonies happen."

"I can't stay," Georgian interjected as he walked away from the others.

"Your conference is at nearly the same time as my birthday," said Whip.

Bully Bravo cocked his head.

"My advisors have a ceremony planned for my eighteenth birthday... elsewhere. What kind, they won't tell me. Just that it will be unforgettable."

"Congratulations." Bully then continued to press his point. "About the ships?"

"They're still under construction," Genghis once again interceded. "When they're ready to be deployed, you'll know about it."

"You came in on one of them, didn't you," said Bravo, with the serious expression of a man who recognizes a fearsome danger. "I got a good look at the Godspeed when you dropped into orbit. You based your design on Zarawti, the space shark that Erlik built?"

"It's one of nature's designs," said Genghis. "It will revolutionize ship-building."

"An Earth starship with a flexible body design is certainly new," said Bravo. "Yours won't have an appetite, will they?"

"We're here to offer our goodwill to the Wild Stars elite," said Whip.

"I wouldn't call them elite," Bravo smiled and shook a hesitant Whip's hand. "But by Earth standards, I can see how they'd give that impression. Speaking of impressions. Didn't you just come from Earth? Didn't you get the distress calls?"

"Distress calls?" Whip looked at Genghis, while trying to surreptitiously wipe his palm on his clothing, having rarely been exposed to physical contact with others.

"We suffered a communications breakdown,"

Genghis stated flatly.

"Better get that fixed before you leave."

Bully Bravo thanked Whip in advance for the Artomique's future assistance with the crisis, and offered to escort them. But other new arrivals had recognized him at that point.

"Thanks for the offer, but I plan on walking there," Whip waved Bully on. "I want to know more about Wild Stars culture."

"There's danger in this," Genghis whispered.

"That's why you're here," Whip replied as he exited the aerodrome and was too surprised to find a bustling community clustered all about. He stood motionless for some time, taking in the sights of an alien world. "Why didn't you tell me about the pirates? I saw you deactivating those distress signals."

"Pirates know better than to tangle with an Artomique class starship," Genghis replied. "But we were already late for your meeting with the Terraformers."

"And what about our duty by Interstellar Law?"

"Soon you'll be the one writing those laws," said Georgian as he rejoined them, having recovered his diplomatic case from customs.

"That's right," Whip replied.

"Never say or think that," Genghis admonished. "Don't even think about our plans for the future. None of us. Not here. Not now."

Georgian nodded in response to the rebuke. There was a clear but unspoken order of rank between his mentors.

"That won't be hard for me," Whip stepped away in the direction of the main thoroughfare, "since you've both kept me in the dark on most of those plans."

Keeping the biggest building off in the distance constantly in sight, Whip walked the streets feeling like he was a butterfly. His feet seemed to barely touch the ground as he crossed and recrossed streets whenever something more interesting would catch his attention on each block of the city that was laid out in a grid pattern, much like communities on Earth.

When Whip saw several men entering a small

shop and leaving with what looked like loaves of bread, what caught his attention were the thrilled looks on their faces and how they clutched the long paper bags to their chests like prized possessions.

Whip entered the shop.

"I'm from Earth," he introduced himself to the man working the counter. "What is it you sell?"

The clerk gave him a blank look, reached inside a drawer, and pulled out a small plug similar to the universal translator Whip wore in his ear. The clerk inserted it and motioned for Whip to repeat his question.

"What is it you sell?"

"It depends," he replied. "What do you like? I don't have any grak or straculum, which, from looking at you, is what you're probably used to."

The clerk's words were mostly echoed in English, although some of the words that Whip thought unique were not translated, meaning that they were already considered part of Terran linguistics.

"Or do you want to try something different?"

"I'll go with your advice," said Whip. "What's the price?"

"One ounce of gold."

The translation seemed excessive to Whip.

"Could you repeat that?"

The clerk stopped his motion of placing in a paper bag what looked like a fresh-baked loaf of bread, with a marbled exterior sprinkled over by shiny spices.

"If you want grak and straculum," the clerk replied, "they sell that across the street."

"Sorry. No insult intended. I'm not familiar with how trade works in the Wild Stars. So I take it that there are no set scales on trade."

The clerk tapped his earplug.

"A monetary system." Whip held up his hand to pay electronically with the chip inserted there.

The clerk looked confused, held up his own hand with the palm out, and then lightly slapped Whip's palm. When he saw Whip's confusion, the clerk shrugged his shoulders.

"How do I pay?" Whip pressed.

"Silver is nice. Gold is better. Reputation is everything."

Whip found some United States coinage mixed with Caribbean in one of his pockets, and offered them all.

"Reputation?" Whip asked as the clerk ran his index fingers over the coins being offered, hesitating for only a second over the pennies.

"Not everything is done for silver and gold." The clerk looked down at the half-bagged loaf and back at Whip. "But between you and me? I don't know you, so I'm going to need to see some gold."

"What about credit?"

"I've already told you," the clerk's mood began to have an edge. "I don't know you, and you don't have a reputation."

"My mistake. I won't repeat it."

Genghis looked at Whip's empty hands when he rejoined him outside.

"What was that about?" he asked.

"Learning how things work in the Wild Stars."

"In the Wild Stars," said Georgian, "people still work for reward, unlike Earth. Since the orbital solar collector has supplied all of Earth's power, almost no one actually does anything that would be considered labor. Our automatons do."

"As long as they don't rebel again," Whip interjected.

"They're all programmed now with minimal intelligence. Earth's populations are supported by the governments. Sure, there are careers for people who are more goal-orientated, and there will never not be a need for soldiers, but most people live a life of leisure and self-indulgence."

"That's why they became so addicted to Whisper Ice Cream," said Whip. "Now they're all sheep being herded around by laser monkeys. And not everyone lives in similar conditions. Daily protests prove that it's not an ideal life."

"It's all good for business," said Georgian.

"The Wild Stars are a capitalist system," Genghis shrugged, "and not, at the same time. You don't have the kind of government oversight like we have over everything on Earth. Even more surprising, no one takes advantage of it."

"Ripe for the pickings?" Whip knew his comment would draw a smile from Genghis. He had given the response expected from a descendant of Achilles Hister. But at his core, he questioned the justification of inflicting predatory practices on an easily victimized population. That the Artomique Corporation had grown into a world power by doing this for nearly two hundred years was his heritage, but he had begun to question whether it had to be his personal legacy.

"True," said Genghis. "But, again, let's stop all thoughts like that for now."

That was when Whip realized how what he had come to do was out of character.

"Peace with the Wild Stars?" he asked Genghis, then turned to Georgian. "A galaxy in harmony? How do those things give us an advantage."

"It's a long term plan," Georgian replied. "Trust us. Just as we applied the Artomique Paradigm to Earth, we do the same in the stars."

"You've both been good mentors, but my eighteenth birthday is in two days. When I assume full control over the Artomique Corporation, it'll be time for you both to become a bit more forthright."

"We will," Genghis replied.

"When it's time," Georgian concluded. "You will understand everything."

"That time is almost here." Whip wondered why his words seemed to bother Georgian, while Genghis was unfazed. Whip had always felt a closer bond with Georgian, and he thought his mentors' reactions would have been reversed.

As they stepped onto the stone steps of the building where their meeting with Erlik and the other decision-makers of the Wild Stars would take place, Genghis and Georgian each grabbed one of Whip's arms at the same time.

Climbing the steps directly in front of them, heading in the same direction, was the man they had seen fighting in the nebula wreckage. Judging by how he had previously disappeared and had now somehow arrived on Ansa before their ultra-swift dreadnought, President Bully Bravo's illegitimate son appeared to have just confirmed that he had the ability to move through time and space.

The Wild Stars were proving to be a much greater danger to the Artomique Paradigm than Whip had ever imagined possible, and his imagination had been running in overdrive.

Chapter Three:
Who Owns Earth?

Bullson knew how disconcerting it was for others when a time traveler would appear from nowhere, and so he returned to the bustling street traffic on Ansa, where he emerged from the anonymity of the crowd and climbed the stone steps to the newly constructed parliament building.

It was a magnificent structure that Earthmen thought reflected a Greek influence, with marble columns lining the exterior. But Bullson knew it was the Greeks who had been influenced by the Wild Stars. Everything was built of intricately cut stone that interlocked so tightly no mortar was required. Not even a sheet of paper could fit into the non-existent gaps of the joints. It was trimmed with the same white marble as the columns.

When he entered the main council chamber, Bullson saw Risky Bravo leaning on the lectern in the center of the speaker's floor. Also known as Tomas Shawnee, Risky was the father of Bully Shawnee, whom Bullson had recruited to help defeat the Saturnian-Eybontic hybrid, Dalucar. Bullson was surprised to see Risky's clone body not only fully revived and moving about, but doing so with great agitation. He spoke very loudly as he addressed the dark-haired Erlik, who was outfitted as always in his Wild Stars armor, and the few others that occupied the seats around a semi-circle table.

"Miri, Akara's World, Magus IV," Risky concluded with a shortness of breath that revealed a newborn body with no physical endurance, "whatever you want to call it, deserves to be left to its own devices!"

"Would you like to address this?" Erlik looked in Bullson's direction just as a hand patted his shoulder.

"I'd be happy to," Admiral Bryce walked past Bullson, picking up a chair and carrying it with him down the main aisle. He offered Risky a seat before he joined Erlik at the council table. "You're looking a lot better than the last time I saw you."

"Miri is a Wild Stars world that was left behind," Erlik elucidated, "because we always felt that those who lived there should be allowed to pursue their preferred primitive lifestyles."

Bryce nodded. He was a short but stout man, his body reflecting a lifetime spent mostly in space.

"Yes," he said, "and I'll be the first to acknowledge that Earth did a lot of damage when previous administrations tried to colonize it."

"And later abandoned it," said Risky. "So, why are you now trying to return to Miri? Keep Miri out of this whole unification of Earth and the Wild Stars."

"There has been no return authorized by President Perez," said Bryce. "And, before him, President Bravo outlawed Akaran wood and all exports from the planet. You're telling me that's changed?"

"Yes," said Risky. "I've been contacted by the Tiberals, who've..."

"The Tiberals?" Erlik interjected. "When did they learn to use MagLink technology?"

"They've learned a lot of new things after repeated invasions from Earth and the Brothan," Risky replied. "Earth abandoned Miri, Akara's World, when they thought it was about to be destroyed by a Marzanti spike. It wasn't, and now you Black Eyes are coming back."

"Let me guess," said Bryce. "Diamond hunters. I have heard reports that they've had some gruesome encounters with dire griefs."

"Among others," Risky replied. "The tree harvesters are back, too. Enough for the Tiberals to declare war on Earth."

"What?" Bryce and Erlik said almost simultaneously.

"Isn't that like a mouse challenging a lion?" Bryce added to his reaction.

"They've already been joined by the Brudwata," Risky rejoined, "and believe you me, they are the most formidable fighters you'll ever meet. They might even give my son trouble in hand-to-hand combat."

As the conversation about the rights and needs of the primitive world heated up, Bullson paid more attention this time when he heard the chamber door open behind him. He noticed how Achilles Hister entered with a special type of gravity around him, accustomed to everything and everyone responding to his will. Bullson also noticed the uncomfortable way that Achilles and his henchmen looked at him, and he knew that the men had recently encountered President Bravo. He could smell his father on them. But surrounded by a room of telepaths, Bullson knew to keep his powers in check, lest he reveal more about himself than he was ready to. So, he probed only slightly into the minds of the Earthmen—no more than what anyone else in the room would do when encountering strangers—and noticed a lot of other fingerprints touching their minds at the very same time.

"I don't usually see you smile like that," said Bullson's father, Bully Bravo, as he entered the room right behind the Artomique Corp representatives. When Daestar, Erlik's wife, entered behind him, Bravo added, "... except when there is a pretty woman present."

Daestar was easily the most formidable telepath that Bullson had ever encountered, outside of his own God Mother. Reading the whole room in a glance, she quickly determined that the urgent matter on her mind should wait and moved to join Erlik's daughter, Akara, in the gallery where she sat with her husband, the clone of some Earthman named Carlton MacKanaly who had lived hundreds of years before.

Bullson let his smile fade—not because of his jealousy over the beautiful Akara's affection for her husband. It was because of the reaction he had read in Achilles's mind toward his father's comment. While Achilles considered Daestar to be an attractive woman, he also considered her too old.

Insulted by what he had read, Bullson certified the young Achilles to be a complete fool and lost respect for the man who was not that much younger than himself, so he pushed deeper into the Earthman's thoughts.

He discovered how Achilles and both of his companions recognized Bullson, even though they had never met. When he probed even deeper, Bullson realized that these Artomiques had been watching on a nearby ship when he and Bully Shawnee battled the Eybontic-Saturnian hybrid Dalucar on the wreckage of the Marzanti ship. But these Artomiques seemed to have no inkling about how Shawnee had then left the galaxy and were startled that Bullson could have arrived on Ansa before them.

Bullson snorted his disappointment. He had expected more. He did not even bother trying to figure what it was that made the Artomiques so happy to see Risky Bravo.

Erlik gave Bullson a quick cut of his eyes, obvious from across the room as he paused the discussion with Risky. He then rose to greet Achilles with a handshake after Bully Bravo entered the hall and led the Artomiques onto the speaker's floor.

"I'll get right to the point," said Achilles as he gestured to Georgian Raveling to set his briefcase on the council table.

Erlik motioned for him to stop before Georgian opened it.

"I agree about getting to the point," said Erlik. "Let's be very open about a few things. I know how your companions have extended your lives through many lifetimes with stolen Wild Stars technology."

Bullson caught Achilles's mind reeling at the mention of their lives being extended, but, at the same time, the boy was not completely surprised. The implication of the extent of Erlik's knowledge was what really shocked the young Artomique.

"How can something be stolen when it's taught to you?" Genghis Champlain countered with a cool and calm demeanor showing both within and without.

"So you admit that the Artomique Corporation was well acquainted with Vic, the clone of my late brother, Vickerus, around the time of Earth's millennial turn?"

"He was Earth's architect in the art of cloning," Achilles conceded to the chagrin of his companions.

"I was there, two hundred years ago, at Earth's Wild Stars outpost when the Brothan bombed it from space," said Erlik. "All those cloning chambers had to have been destroyed."

"Vic had another one stored in a vault in the Granite Rock Bank vault," Achilles replied. "Not even Carthage and the Brothan dropping the entire building could damage it."

"What happened to Vic?" Erlik demanded more than asked.

"According to our records," said Achilles, "Vic only chose to regenerate one more time."

Bullson caught a flash in Genghis's mind; a memory of standing next to the cloning chamber as Vic stepped out—only to be shot in the head. But that had happened nearly two hundred years ago, lending credence to Erlik's earlier statement about the Artomiques employing life extensions. These Earthmen were gradually becoming more interesting to him.

"But at least he was able to teach us the technology," Achilles added.

Bullson wondered why Erlik did not notice Achilles's deceit, but then began to suspect that maybe he had.

"What is this important matter of the Wild Stars that you wanted to know?" Erlik asked.

"This." Achilles gestured to Georgian to open the case and remove the contents—an egg-shaped object that looked very much like lapis lazuli stone with an engraved golden band around the center—which he displayed to everyone seated at the table. "I believe you call this an Icarus stone. According to the engraving—it gives me ownership of the Earth."

"How do you imagine that?" asked Erlik.

Achilles showed only a single twitch of surprise at this response.

"Whoever possesses the Icarus stone owns the Earth."

"Like this?"

Erlik leaned across the table and snatched the stone out of Georgian's hand. He then passed the stone back across the table to Bullson, who had continued to hover near the Earthmen. Understanding what Erlik was doing, Bullson handed the stone to his father, who then passed it back across the table to Bryce, who returned it to Erlik.

"How's the wife?" Erlik asked in a cavalier manner.

"Veranda is good," Bryce replied.

Achilles made a hand motion, indicating for his companions not to react to these theatrics, while his face betrayed an anger that he seemed unaccustomed to dealing with.

"I thought the leaders of the Wild Stars were known for a code of honor?" asked Achilles. "Either you are very poor at humor or a thief."

"You expected to come here and start dictating terms to me, all because you were holding this a moment ago?" Erlik raised the stone to eye level. "That this made you the owner of Earth? Earth is a responsibility, and mine is making sure that someone like you doesn't have it."

"Someone like me?" Achilles growled. "You don't know me. We've never met."

"You Artomiques infiltrated the Granite Rock Bank before it was even destroyed, and then you took advantage, looted the vault and made Vic into your prisoner. Who's the thief now?" He looked around at the other men who had just held the stone. "Besides, by your own argument of possession establishing ownership, there now appears to be a questionable chain of possession."

"Where would you get such an idea?" asked Genghis.

"From you," Bullson interjected to everyone's surprise.

"You've had your way on Earth for a long time," Erlik pointed at Achilles between the eyes. "But the people who remained on Earth didn't have all the inherent abilities that come naturally to many in the Wild Stars. Despite your massive corporate resources built on stolen Wild Stars technology, you have no training in dealing with telepathy."

"Every person here can read your mind like you would read faces," said Bullson. "No body language control can disguise your actual self—what's inside you."

"You and your men are babes in the stars," said Erlik. "Go back to Earth and stay out of the Wild Stars. Be happy with the empire you've built on theft." He once again hefted the Icarus stone. "Even though this is nothing more than a symbolic bauble, you're leaving it here. It was never yours to begin with."

Achilles lunged forward and snatched the stone back.

Erlik could have easily kept the Artomique from grabbing it, but Bullson could see his curiosity about what the Earthman planned to do next.

"You're right," Achilles held the stone high, doing a semi-turn to show it off to the scattered spectators sitting about the gallery, "I *am* leaving it here."

He handed the stone to Risky, who still sat nearby in the chair Bryce had brought.

The reborn man looked quite startled.

"Why give it to me?" he asked.

"Because you're the only one here," Achilles glowered first at former President Bully Bravo and then Admiral Bryce, "that I consider to be a *true* Earthman."

Genghis and Georgian exchanged a grin and a nod of satisfaction.

"I came to return this," Achilles patted the stone one last time, "but an event this momentous deserves more pomp and circumstance than I have time for. I ask you, Mister Risky Bravo, will you officially return the Icarus Stone to the Wild Stars during the upcoming conference?"

"Wait a minute," said Risky. "I'm here to complain about Earth. Not represent it."

"That doesn't represent Earth." Achilles and his companions turned and headed for the door. Halfway up the aisle, Achilles paused and turned. "After all, as Erlik said, it's nothing more than a bauble. Earth belongs to Earth, no matter what any engraving on a rock says."

"I think every government on Earth will agree with him," said Bully Bravo.

Strange young man, thought Bullson. *Erlik will use the stone as a symbol of Earth having always been a part of the Wild Stars.*

It seemed to be a very poor tactical move on the part of the Artomiques.

Chapter Four:
The Red Queen Returns

The Artomique dreadnought class starship powered out of Ansa's orbit and set a direct course for the Orbital MagLink Relay Center.

"There are some things I don't understand," Whip said to his advisors as they gathered in the observation lounge.

"Erlik is a son of the Ancient Warrior," said Georgian, "and the whole family is a pack of liars. They'll say anything to advance the notion that the Wild Stars provide a superior way of life and that they are the pinnacles of how that life should be lived."

"There's no truth to his accusation about us extending our lives," said Genghis. "If either Georgian or I had been alive for 200 years, would we even consider relinquishing control of the empire that we'd built with that time?"

Whip nodded at the logic of their words.

"Still," he said, "I don't understand why you wanted me to give them the Icarus stone?"

"It's simple," Genghis replied. "What do you think will happen when they try to assert ownership over Earth based on their possession of a rock no one has ever heard of before?"

"No one will take them seriously," Whip concluded.

"Exactly," said Georgian. "They want to bring Earth and all its star-flung colonies under the Wild Stars umbrella. When Earth refuses to be lorded over, the colonies will follow suit."

"Why didn't my father deal with any of this? He's still officially the head of the corporation. And what about all this recent pirate activity?"

"We'll deal with all that once we reach the Relay Center," Genghis asserted.

Push as he might, Whip could get neither of his advisors to reveal more.

Desperate for answers, Whip returned to his laboratory and unlocked the safe holding the Eybontic head. Once his firewalls were secure, he powered it back up.

"Carthage?" he asked when the eyes began to glow.

"Yeah, that's me," the voice box responded.

"What do you know about the pirate's Red Queen?"

"Which one?"

"What do you mean?" Whip found the answer puzzling.

"Which Red Queen?"

"There's more than one?"

"Of course. How do you think the pirates were able to always keep Earth's military away? The pirates work every angle: the colonies, the Terraformers, and more things on Earth than you would ever suspect."

"You're being evasive," Whip observed, "almost like you're stalling with your answers. What did you tell me last time?"

When there was a hesitation with the answer, Whip instantly disconnected the power source.

"Dalucar," he stated his fear aloud and ran a systems check for any abnormal activity. He knew that the Saturnians could free their consciousness and surf the digital world of operating and artificial intelligence interfaces.

Even when he found no trace of activity, Whip still worried that he might have unintentionally released the monster from its prison. His hands trembled as he replaced the head in the safe and locked it away, vowing to never open it again.

Over the rest of the day's journey to the Orbital MagLink Relay Center, Whip kept his fears private, but he continued to check and recheck every system on the dreadnought, looking for even the slightest abnormalities.

His attention on the trigger alarms he had placed on all key systems heightened when an image of the space station appeared on the observation lounge's main screen as their destination neared.

Once the dreadnought dropped from hyper-light speed, all the portals and observation screens on the ship switched to live views of local space.

The station was lined with massive, ringed compartments that were connected to a central spire, and interspersed with rows of fat, commercial hub spires that looked like clubs because of the way they fattened farther away from the center section, where traffic poured in and out. The Orbital MagLink Relay Station slowly spun about as it orbited Sword, an uninhabitable super-Earth six times the size of Terra. Four times was the maximum number of multiple Earth gravities that a human could survive without the assistance of exo-gear, and the world remained unexplored except by robot crafts that invariably seemed to malfunction, giving the planet the reputation of being haunted.

Sword itself orbited the sun Damocles, which had recently begun showing signs of instability. Adding to the mystery of Sword was the fact that it had a chemical composition that did not match with its host star. If not for its ideal location for a MagLink relay, no space station would ever have been put in orbit. Everyone who passed through the station knew a fatal act of force majeure could happen at any moment, giving even more reason not to bother exploring the planet below.

As Whip disembarked on the gateway linked to a side hatchway on the dreadnought, the remote control pad he carried in his pocket gave a single blip. His advisors looked at him with confusion when he nervously inspected the readings, but he quickly determined that it was simply a systems interface with one of the station's automated service droids.

"Anything amiss?" asked Georgian.

"Maintenance alert." Whip shook his head as they exited the corridor, and took a surprised look around at the luxurious furnishings of the lounge they entered. There were no customs agents or processing centers. It looked more like another executive lounge, where beautiful and scantily clad women gathered around an open bar and smiled in his direction.

"This isn't a military processing center," said Whip, "like dreadnoughts normally dock at."

"No," Genghis grabbed Whip's arm when he started to detour toward the feminine distractions.

"This gateway is for royalty and high-level diplomats," said Georgian, "which is how you will soon be considered."

"Today's the day," Whip affirmed his impending ascension to control over the corporation. He pulled his attention from the flirtatious women. "Where *is* father?"

"He's waiting at the ceremony," Genghis guided Whip only a few steps down the main corridor before they stopped at an interior conference room.

Whip felt a moment of trepidation as they stepped into a darkened room. When the lights rose, he realized his instincts were right.

Several armed men were waiting just inside, but they were not dressed in military attire. Their clothing was a mishmash of civilian cultures.

"Pirates," he quickly surmised.

Neither Genghis nor Georgian seemed concerned when Whip turned to them. Georgian pointed to the table in the center of the large conference room, at the far end of which sat an unusual woman.

"Meet the Red Queen," he said.

"Mister Hister, I can see your disappointment," the red-headed woman leaned back in the enormous, ornately carved wooden seat with a high and wide back that made it look more like a throne than a chair. She pulled both sides of the black cloak she wore tightly around her neck, covering her ample bosom, where Whip's eyes had instantly dropped. "You were expecting something different?"

"Does everyone in the stars read minds?" asked Whip. In many ways, this woman reminded him of Daestar—attractive for a middle-aged woman with a look in her eyes that hinted she knew more about him than he did about himself.

"No," the Red Queen replied. "But everyone you've met recently does. For a man who has lived many lives making and executing intricate, long-term plans, you came into the stars remarkably unprepared. You don't know what you're doing. I don't understand how you caused my late sister, Scarlet, so much trouble."

"Nefarimor?"

"Yes, I can see now that you are beginning to realize how much danger you are in. You and she were rivals, but you've always wanted to be my ally. Did you really never suspect that you already were? Or that Scarlet and I were not just sisters who were partners—we were interchangeable. We exchanged places often. So I already know you well enough."

"Excuse me," said Whip, "but I do not know you. Never knew a Scarlet Tanager. Heard of her. Heiress to the Whisper Ice Cream fortune before the whole company crashed when its secret ingredient was revealed to be poison. But never met her."

"Little fool, who thought you could reshape the world, my grandiloquence wasn't just for you," said the matriarch. "I was talking to both you and your father."

Achilles Hister the 7th stepped out from behind the Red Queen's chair. He was dressed in a black uniform and leather jacket that Whip recognized as being an alternate-reality Artomique design. His eyes were shadowed by the brim of his hat, but still shined with intensity—and showed no hint of love.

"He will soon be you," said the Red Queen.

"Hello, son," said the elder Achilles. "Time to say goodbye."

Chapter Five: A Stolen Life

"Our children have left Miri," Daestar told Erlik moments after the Artomiques had departed.

"Where would they go?" Erlik asked.

"They're probably trying to defend their home," Risky Bravo stood up, but quickly leaned against the lectern, "just like I'm trying to do."

"It's worse than that," said Daestar.

"Worse than a world in danger?" Risky admonished.

"For them it is," Daestar asserted, and focused on her next words to Erlik. "There are things that I've never told you before, about a secret organization of telepaths that has embedded itself into the Wild Stars for millennia. I was a member before we first met."

Erlik seemed stunned for a moment, weighing his next words.

"This has something to do with my mother," he finally spoke, "doesn't it?"

"Probably," Daestar replied. "I'm not sure. All I know is I overheard Risky's nurse talking about them going to a place called the Orbital MagLink Relay Center."

"*My* nurse?" asked Risky. "From the cloning?"

"What is this group called?" asked Erlik.

"She helped with your mental transference," Daestar answered Risky, and turned to Erlik. "They, we, are called the Five Thousand Fingered Hand, because we are many and everywhere, always operating in secret."

"Why didn't you tell me this before?" asked Erlik.

"Because of what happened to your mother," Daestar then glanced at Akara, still sitting in the gallery, "and your daughter's hatred of telepaths because of it. But we can discuss all that later. Right now, our children are in danger."

"From the Five Thousand Fingered Hand?" Erlik asked. "You're afraid they'll try to exert influence on our children, like my mother tried to influence my father."

"I'm not sure," said Daestar. "But I don't trust them. I need to go where they're headed and stop them."

"I'll go with you," said Bully Bravo.

"Shouldn't you stay here?" asked Daestar. "Help establish a relationship between the Wild Stars and Earth?"

"As you might have noticed by the way that young Mister Hister looked at me," said Bully, "there is a chance that I could be seen as a distraction. Besides, where you're going isn't that far away. We should have plenty of time to get there and get back again before the conference starts. I've found that sometimes it's best to first let people argue themselves out and then come in near the end to close things up."

Erlik shrugged.

"I can't leave right now, and I'd appreciate knowing that someone both trustworthy and capable went with you."

"We can double down on that capable part," said Bravo. "I'll ask Bullson to come with us. Give us a little bonding time with a mutual purpose."

But when Bravo looked about for his son, he was nowhere to be seen.

"He was right there," said Admiral Bryce. "He must have just disappeared out the door."

"Guess it's just the two of us," shrugged Bravo.

"With the way Bullson looks at me," said Daestar, "and just about every other woman he sees, maybe that's not a bad thing."

"I wanted to ask him how his mission to recover and relocate Ruin went," said Bravo. "There's no way that they could have accomplished all that and been back so soon. And if he's back, where are Tall

Trees and my nephew?"

"Don't worry about it, and just stay safe," said Risky. "I'm supposed to be the brother who does all the crazy things."

"Take a Wild Stars scout ship," said Erlik. "It's the fastest ship there is."

After attending to several quick matters, Bravo joined Daestar for what he declared would be the shortest star journey either of them had ever taken. He then suggested that they both try to sleep through the journey in their chairs, since the Wild Stars scout ship would arrive at the Orbital MagLink Center right at the start of their daytime cycle.

"Looks like some of our friends barely beat us here," Bully Bravo focused on one particular starship as they neared the docking bays, "which is amazing time by the clock speeds of an Earth ship, especially for a rig that big. Despite their head start, I didn't think there was anything that could beat this Wild Stars scout ship here."

"Why is that Artomique dreadnought parked at the diplomatic gate?" asked Daestar.

"The relay center is under Earth's control," Bravo observed. "That just goes to show how much influence the Artomiques have these days. They've always had their hands into politics, but since I stepped down, they've stepped up. Considering all the uncharacteristic moves that he's made since then, I think Perez is in their pocket."

"Looks like we're going through customs with everyone else," Daestar remarked as their ship's controls were taken over remotely and they were guided through the magnetized opening on the fat end of a commercial hub at the very bottom of the station.

"Looks like we're going to be walking," said Bravo. "Hope the Sword of Damocles doesn't fall soon."

Daestar wondered about his comment but chose not to search his mind for an answer.

As they disembarked, the customs officer approaching them was suddenly distracted by a notification he received on his info pad. He ran a stylus across his information pad several times, each

time more excited than the one before.

"What's happened?" asked Bravo.

"The news just broke," the officer said, "that the Maxitrillion Warship fighting with that Neth entity in Nebula 71 has been destroyed."

"That *is* bad news," Bravo's jaw set, and his expression changed into one that had earned him the nickname of *the Scary President* early in his political career.

"Only a few Sprinter ships managed to escape. That whole area is being quarantined."

"That's not far from here," Bravo observed, "but I don't think this station needs to worry. Neth is a gaseous creature, and without a ship, he's not going to trouble anyone. That's why they implemented a quarantine."

"How could you know any of..." the officer looked up from his pad and instantly recognized the former President. "I'm so sorry, Sir! No one told me you were coming." He waved them past. "Why weren't you routed through the diplomatic wing?"

"It was busy."

The officer quickly became distracted again.

The scout ship had been parked next to a junker, whose owners were embroiled in a loud argument with a local merchant.

"This is the second time that this has happened!" the captain shouted, showing great animation in both voice and body language.

The merchant, dressed in a monochrome suit of plain design, cowered and shielded his face.

"We'll pay you anything you want," he begged.

"Except what you agreed!" the ship's captain argued back, but unclenched his fist when he saw the port authority officer watching. "You know what we came for! We don't get it, you don't get either the beer or the gold."

"But pirates stole it in transit," the merchant pleaded. "A coupling that big could power a whole planet. We put on extra security and even asked the military to help, but they wouldn't. The pirates got it. What else can we offer you for the beer? More gold?"

"I've already got gold!" The captain snorted and turned to talk privately with his two crew members.

One was a young woman, and the other was someone who surprised Bravo when his face turned to where it could be seen.

"Wild Child!" Bravo called out.

The man's eyes grew wide when he in turn recognized Bravo, but he immediately hand-signaled with downward palms for Bravo to stay quiet, shaking his head as though they did not know each other.

"Isn't that Lonan Mcguffin, the Terraformer heir?" asked Daestar. "I thought he disappeared on his way home to take over the family business."

"Saw his cousin, Josette, on Ansa just the other day," said Bravo. "My guess is that she's the one he's really trying to avoid."

Daestar gave the young man the briefest of probes and then nodded her confirmation of Bravo's suspicion.

"Who would have thought that a junker captain would turn his nose up at an offer of gold," said Bravo. "If he's got a cargo-hold of beer, he can name his price. With so many people suffering from Mcguffinut withdrawal, it's one of the few things that relieves the symptoms."

"That crew wants something specific," said Daestar.

They proceeded to walk the length of the commercial hub in silence, each taking in all the chatter and activity happening around them. Once they came to a moving walkway, they rode it all the way to the main concourse.

Bully looked right, then left.

"I guess we go up," said Bravo. "Just how are we supposed to find your children on a station this big? They could be anywhere."

"If they're around," said Daestar, "I'll find them."

"Oh, right," Bully conceded. "I've heard about your special *skills*. All right, lead the way. I've got your back."

Bravo took several steps on the winding upward tilt of the concourse before he realized that Daestar had not moved.

She stood staring in the opposite direction.

"Down there is only the main engine compartment," Bully explained. "Unless your kids are engineers, you won't find them there."

"It's not them," Daestar replied as several badge-wearing workers exited onto the main concourse through the locked door that led to the station's engine rooms. She watched them closely as they passed, lost in conversation. "I sense the presence of a dire grief, hiding aboard nearby. And it's not just that. It's what those two men we just passed are working on. Those power couplings that Mcguffin's friends were looking for? I think I found one of them. Why would anyone want to build a gravity elevator to a planet no one can visit?"

"That doesn't make a lick of sense," said Bravo. "Neither part. What would a dire grief be doing away from Akara's World? And no one builds a space elevator to a 6G world. What would make you think that?"

"It's what *they* were thinking about." Daestar pointed at the engineers. "Special skills, remember?"

"I'm beginning to understand," said Bully. "Let's concentrate on finding your children, and we'll try to figure out that other stuff later."

"Trust me. I know what I'm talking about."

"I don't doubt it. First things first."

They spent an entire morning cycle winding their way up the massive station's main spire, exploring every ring and stopping at cafes for the occasional meal and to rest. By the afternoon cycle, they were no longer bypassing the conveyor walks. When the dimming of the concourse lights signaled the start of the station's evening cycle, they had reached the very top.

Bully Bravo was once again recognized by the station security staff, and they were allowed into the executive level.

"Think we'll find them here?"

"It's the only place left to look," Daestar replied.

Daestar passed the doors to a conference room, then she stopped suddenly.

"Is it them?" Bravo asked.

Daestar shook her head.

"Something's wrong here," she put a hand on the door latch and discovered it unlocked.

Together they entered the darkened room, with Daestar standing in the sliver of illumination cast by the concourse while Bravo searched for the light switches. When he found them, the light revealed a single occupant, sitting in an over-sized wooden chair on the far end of a large conference table.

"Bully Bravo," the man in his mid-fifties looked up from an apparent slumber, but when he tried to move, it became obvious that his hands were bound to the arms of the chair.

"Achilles Hister," Bravo said with surprise, "the 7th!"

"The 8th!" he protested.

"I just saw the 8th the other day," Bravo argued as he moved to untie the bonds, "and he's a whole lot younger than you."

"You're Daestar," Whip said as he was released. "I saw you on Ansa, too. What's been done to me? This isn't my body!"

Daestar was startled, pausing a moment to look deep into Hister's eyes. His mind opened so easily that the slightest mental push felt like she had reached nearly all the way into his soul. She quickly broke contact and looked around the room for something that she could not find.

"Were there any others here?" she asked.

"Why would anyone do something like this?" he asked in reply. "If someone wants a new body, just grow one. We've got the technology. Why steal mine?"

"Cloning isn't the clean system you'd think it is," she replied. "My son-in-law was recently transferred into a cloned body."

"I met him, remember? Tomas Shawnee, the man some called Risky. Why do people take so many names in the Wild Stars? It gets complicated. I gave him the Icarus stone."

"My name is Daestar. As uncomplicated as it gets. What's yours?"

"I prefer Whip."

"Your real name."

"Achilles Hister the 8th. But Whip is what my teachers used to call me."

"Sharp as a Whip," Daestar replied with a smile. "And just as quick."

"I don't understand—what's happened to me?"

"With a clone body, it takes some time for a mind to connect with muscles that have never been used. And a clone body initially has no natural immunities or personal bacterial biome. So there's an adjustment period that you don't have with a body that was grown naturally—one that has already been processed through all that growth."

"It's so cruel—a violation of body and soul!"

"That's why it's forbidden."

"Why does it make you so angry?" Whip was incredulous about her evident sympathy. He no longer trusted anyone.

"Because if they'd do this with you, the heir to the Artomique hierarchy, then they'll this to anyone. I came looking for my children. With their already enhanced skills of telepathy, they would be perfect candidates for an aged telepath. And believe me, those who control the Five Thousand Fingered Hand do not lightly give up power. Obviously, forbidden things are accepted in this day and age."

"Wait," said Bravo. "You're saying that you believe him? That this really is Achilles the 8th?"

"In the body of the 7th," Daestar confirmed.

"What are their names?" Whip asked.

"I've been gone for some time. I'm sure the Hand is ruled by others now."

"No. What are the names of your children?"

"Akarastar and Mackstar."

"I'd always wondered why I had no brothers or sisters. I'll help you find your children."

Daestar could not stop her smile.

"I think we're the ones who need to be helping you," she replied. "Who did this?"

"My father," Whip replied. "Achilles Hister the 7th."

"He must be a man of pure evil to do that to his own son—just to avoid a few months of rehabilitation," said Daestar. "What are we going to do with him?"

"Let's get him out of here." Bravo took Whip by the arm and started walking him toward the door.

"Won't father's men try to stop us?" Whip asked.

"I doubt that stealing his son's body is something that he informed station security about," Bravo led the way onto the main concourse and straight to the executive elevator.

The security guards on either side of the elevator doors made no reaction as Whip, Bravo, and Daestar entered the chamber and selected a drop to the lowest level.

"See?" Bravo quipped with a rare smile.

Then the doors opened onto the commercial hub, and his "scary President" expression returned.

Chapter Six:
The Architect of Tomorrow

Bullson merged into the crowds when he appeared on the Orbital MagLink Relay Center, but there was nothing relaxed about this arrival. He hit the ground with a fast first step as people were all moving rapidly in one direction, drawn to a heated discussion that made no sense to most of them.

Having keyed his arrival to the first elevated moment of his father's life signs, Bullson was certain that he would find Bully Bravo at the center of whatever confrontation was taking place.

He was not wrong.

"Move these people back!" A lead security guard triggered a warning display of sparks from his club, inducing the crowd to stop and slowly back away from the cluster of people near the executive elevators. He took one look at Bullson, who played a simple trick on the man's mind to make him think that he was looking at another guard. Bullson soon found himself inside the perimeter as it expanded past him.

The Artomiques that he had just seen moments earlier on Ansa were now conversing with Bully Bravo, Daestar, and what looked to be the father of Achilles Hister. His son and his mentors did not appear happy, and they were instructing the guards to aim their weapons.

Bullson approached the aggressors from the rear, intent on surprise. But he was the one surprised when he realized that he was coming in on the middle of the conversation, and the only thing he knew for certain was that the young Hister had suddenly become a far more interesting person.

Bullson paused and focused on Daestar's perspective, trying to decipher what was really happening, while approaching ever more slowly.

"You are a monster," Daestar looked the younger Hister in the eyes, while she and Bully partially shielded the older Hister behind them.

"It's not about rehabilitation," said the younger Hister as he attempted to assert new skills that he had not previously displayed and sensed that Daestar knew he was trying to read her mind.

"There are parts of your personality that get lost when you transfer into a clone," Hister continued. "It could be a favorite food no longer tastes right or other things that seem simple enough. All of which means that, if you transfer enough times, you'll eventually lose something big. Something that is essential to being who you really are."

"How many times have you transferred?"

"That old body was called the 7th for a reason. But I had a theory that being transferred into a naturally cultivated body..."

"Is that what you call stealing the body of your own child?" Daestar could not hide her outrage. "Cultivating?"

"This time I felt none of the fade I'd experienced previously. And except for a few adjustments that still need to be made, I've been fully functional from the moment I took my first step. In fact, I feel strength and drive that my old form had lost. It makes me look at everything differently. Things like you. You're a very attractive woman."

Daestar's face betrayed revulsion mixed with anger.

A loud commotion began to sound nearby in the main parking area, but the Artomiques did not bother to look.

Bullson did not look either, but he could see through the eyes of the elder Hister that a service droid was causing havoc as it moved in their direction.

"You need to get out of here," the elder leaned and whispered to Bully Bravo. "That droid is headed straight for you, and I think it's Dalucar."

Bravo nodded, but seemed unconcerned. He made eye contact with both Daestar and Whip, nodding toward the nearby stacks of empty storage containers on wheeled robotic porters that were waiting to haul them from the cargo sorting area. He seemed to be pointing their attention to a Junker's crew that had just left the main concourse by the customs area on the other side of the cargo area.

"Wait for it," was his only reply.

"You two can go," said Hister to Daestar and Bravo. "Go back and enjoy the Unification Conference on Ansa. But my picture of Dorian Gray stays here."

The younger Hister then noticed that the trio was no longer paying him heed, and he turned to look where their attention had been drawn.

"That's Dalucar," he called out. "The fool set him free! I told you to always keep an eye on whatever he was doing."

As big as a surface-to-space shuttle, the service droid was laboriously working its way in their direction. Despite having only minimal ground traction equipment, its heavy astro-shielding easily deflected the repeated discharges from the security guards' weapons. It moved inexorably forward even as the number of guards continued to increase.

The service droid worked its way near to the semi-circle of guards. Bullson stepped in front of his father as Dalucar approached the Artomiques standing between them.

"Where have you been?" Bravo asked.

"I hate sitting around ships crawling though the cosmos," Bullson replied. "So I took a shortcut."

Bullson drew the turquoise sword hanging at his waist. He took two powerful steps forward, then with a third, he ran up the back of one of Hister's henchmen and leaped into the air.

The service droid raised its many implement-laden arms in a mix of defensive and offensive postures. The turquoise blade cut through them all like they were paper, and then cleaved deep into the droid's head-pan, immediately rendering it motionless.

Before Hister and his men could react, Bullson held his blade out to one side with the point up and approached them with his eyes leveled at theirs.

Both of Hister's companions pulled weapons away from the security guards nearest them, drawing a smile from Bullson.

"Dalucar isn't gone," said Hister. "That droid has too limited an operating system to have contained him. He's still somewhere on this space station."

Hister motioned for all his men to lower their weapons.

"I've heard stories about you," said Hister. "Your name is Bullson."

Bullson stopped, as surprised as Hister's henchmen by the revelation.

"You have no idea who I am," Bullson replied as he gripped the sword hilt with both hands and prepared to rid the universe of another threat, taking one last peek inside the man's mind, with no concern for brute invasiveness.

Then he hesitated.

Bullson began to understand Daestar's previous conversation. Bullson was startled by how much Achilles had changed in the short time since they had first met. From a youth who was virginal like himself when it came to intimacy with women, suddenly he saw a parade of beautiful faces that both shocked and impressed him with the sheer magnitude of the number. It was a staggering collection of memories that was inconceivable for a non-time traveler in such a short time. Having previously only encountered the monogamous and often chaste sexual attitudes of his father and the men and women of the Wild Stars, Bullson found such carnal bounty fascinating.

He finally realized that this Achilles could not be the same person. The mind he now touched had the memories of many lifetimes and formidable defenses against psychic attack. Like a kung fu master who dodges an attack with minimal effort, this new Achilles had allowed Bullson into his mind, always staying right in front of him—and always just beyond his grasp.

Overconfident in his own skills and invulnerability, Bullson became even more captivated by the revelation of Achilles' vision of galactic conquest. Unlike Bullson's father, Bully Bravo, who focused on the more immediate concerns of meliorism, this was a mind that formulated plans for a future that would last for thousands of years.

Here was a true architect of tomorrow.

Too late, a tiny inner voice shouted a faint alarm. Bullson had allowed his mind to be influenced by the desires of a fanatic. His own thought processes began to shut down as his will became subservient in ways he had only experienced as a child—with his God Mother.

"Where did Whip and the others go?" asked one of Hister's men.

"Later," Achilles said, never taking his eyes off Bullson. "We should talk."

Chapter Seven:
Flight of the Gravedigger

The security guards stood around and on top of the Wild Stars scout ship and watched warily when the captain and crew of the salvage ship parked next to it returned with their cargo.

When the captain parked by the dollies loaded with containers just over the yellow line and started to load his own cargo hold, the guard called out a warning.

"Get those things away from this ship!"

"Really?" the captain protested as he walked back. "I've got one wheel over the yellow line, and you're going to run me laps?"

"Just get those as far away from us as you can."

"I'll tell you," the captain continued to grouse, "this has been the day for it." He then went on to harangue the robo-porters working the carts about what an unfair exchange he had accepted for what he was selling.

The robo-porters operated on the lowest level of legal sentience and could provide no reaction.

Once loaded, Junker 7557, aka the Gravedigger according to the port authority tower, was cleared for departure. They were well away into space before Pam Kerk and Lonan Mcguffin opened the cargo containers.

"Thank you, Lonan," said Daestar when she stepped out of her container.

"Just what did you do with all that beer?" Bravo asked as Pam freed him. "That was a lot to give up."

"Don't worry," said Pam. "We've tapped a Lovejoy comet filled with ethyl alcohol and glycolaldehyde. We'll never run out."

"Told the porters to give it away in the community lounge," answered Captain Roy Kerk as he joined them. "Going to be a party on the station tonight that no one will ever forget."

He paused as a frustrated Pam asked for Lonan's help with the last container's lid lock.

"Now, as much as one of you seems to be good friends with Lonan," the captain smiled, "let's everyone introduce ourselves." Once names and pleasantries were exchanged, his expression turned serious. "You made me a promise. Where is my power coupling?"

"The pirates took it," said Daestar, motioning for the captain to calm down when he began to protest that he already knew that. "I know where they took it. To Corsairiana."

The last container's security band released with a pop like a handgun.

The captain blinked.

"How is that supposed to help?"

"No one knows where that is," said Bravo.

"Now you're the one who's not helping," Daestar gave the ex-President a smile. She nodded to Whip as he stepped out of his container. "He knows where it is. Everyone, meet Whip."

Whip looked startled.

"How would I know what?"

The captain threw his hands into the air, and Pam gave Lonan a concerned look and bit her lip.

"Miss Daestar," said Lonan, "we asked all over the station..."

"All day," Pam interjected.

"...and everyone kept telling us the same thing. No one knows where Corsairiana is."

"You may not," Daestar turned back to Whip, "but the man who occupied this body before you, did. There may still be a residual of his knowledge that I can tap."

"You can do that?" asked Bravo.

"If it's there," said Daestar. "As the clone, First Marker learned..." She looked at Bravo. "You know him as Mark Mackavicka. As Mack learned from being a clone, there was residual knowledge somehow transferred over from the donor to him. Now, in

Whip's case, there is no clone process. This was a complete personality exchange. I think it's safe to say that Achilles the 7th won't be anticipating what the possible bleed-through of each your personalities will do to the other."

Everyone else on the ship exchanged blank looks.

"Have a seat," Daestar instructed Whip to sit down in front of her, and she began thoroughly probing his scalp with her fingertips.

"What?" Pam quipped. "Are you getting ready to wash his hair?"

"Looking for pressure points," she replied. Different parts of his body twitched as she touched pressure points. Daestar then stepped back and closed her eyes for a moment.

"So that's why no one could find Corsairiana!" Her eyes snapped back open. "Risky went there, but then couldn't find it again. The reason that no one's ever been able to find it—is because the planet moves! Corsairiana is a planetoid equipped with a planetary engine."

"That would explain why they'd want a power coupling the size of the one they stole," said Roy.

"If their engine is down," said Bravo, "then they're stationary. If we can confirm its position, I can notify Earth's military."

Bravo then paused.

"You folks seem pretty unsurprised to hear about a world with an engine," he observed. "Just how familiar are you with the Wild Stars? What do you want that coupling for?"

There was a moment of nervous silence as no one answered. Daestar decided to break the quiet.

"Show me a star chart."

"Oh, that's a problem." The captain shook his head when she pointed at a section of the image that popped up on the command deck's main forward screen. "That's right on the edge of Nebula 71. That whole area was just quarantined."

"Good," said Bravo. "That means when I make the call, I won't be ignored." He looked again from person to person, but still gained no reaction to his earlier question.

Daestar motioned for Bravo to drop the point, and while the captain and crew discussed the best possible course with the least possibility of a pirate encounter, she pulled Bravo and Whip back down to the cargo hold.

"I need to get access to those controls," Bravo whispered, "and send a recall signal back to the scout ship we abandoned, one with a tag that will help our friends find this ship."

"Why not ask them?" said Daestar.

"These people don't know us, and if I was them, I wouldn't let someone transmit a tracker on my ship." Bravo looked back toward the bridge. "Tell me, what did you learn with your special skills about what they're hiding?"

"I don't know," Daestar answered. "It's shielded in their minds by powerful blocks that I can't get through."

Whip looked increasingly confused by the conversation, and became distracted instead by a rectangular cargo case that was strapped to the wall. He put a hand on the case while reading the manifest stamp, looked down at his own body, and let out an audible sigh.

"So, how many people can do something like that—outside of that Five-Thousand Fingered Hand you told me about?" asked Bravo.

"None—that I know of," Daestar replied. "But I don't sense any malevolent intent from them. Still, Whip here thinks that the pirates and the Hand might be working together, so let's keep it a secret about why we're also interested in going to Corsairiana."

"When did I tell you that?" Whip's attention was brought back to the conversation.

"When we first met," she replied.

Bully tapped a finger to his skull.

"Special skills," he said.

Whip took a startled step back.

"She's like the Red Queen?"

"Yes, and no," Daestar replied.

"She's nothing like the Red Queen," Bravo confirmed. "And what did you think she was doing earlier? When she pulled Corsairiana's location out of your noggin?"

"Give me a break," Whip argued back. "She made me feel like a puppet on a string. I thought maybe with what the Red Queen did to me earlier, that I was somehow broadcasting my thoughts. It's been a rough day, and I'm still trying to wrap my brain around everything that's happened, and it's not even *my* brain!"

"Been a bad day for everyone," said Lonan obliviously as he joined them in the cargo bay, walking straight past to a section of storage lockers on the side wall. "Roy wants the roof cannon fully prepped. Can I get some help installing these quick charge backups?"

Whip stepped forward, but Bravo put a hand on his chest.

"Let someone younger do the heavy lifting." Bravo moved to help Lonan. "I remember when we first met, you were running around butt-naked and half drunk. I've got to say that you don't even seem like the same person. How are you doing with your Mcguffinut withdrawal? You're not showing any symptoms at all."

Bravo reached to unlock an adjacent locker.

Lonan looked up too late. "No! Not that one."

"Damn!" Bravo exclaimed as the hatch swung open to reveal piles of gold bars stacked like bricks. "How much gold do you people have? I should have been a brewer."

Then Bravo's scary president face returned.

"Or... did you scavenge this?"

Chapter Eight:
By the Light of the Lantern Star

"Pam earned that gold," Roy Kerk told Bully Bravo, "pole dancing for drunken miners on the asteroids."

"I did *not*!" His sister stormed off the ship's bridge, past a sympathetic Lonan Mcguffin.

Daestar put a calming hand on Bravo's shoulder when Roy spoke again.

"What business is it of yours, anyway?" he asked. "Didn't you choose not to run for a second term as president because of that video someone released of you decapitating a man on Mars Space Station One? Want to explain that to me?"

"It wasn't a living man—it was a zombie," Bravo replied. "Most of the details are still classified."

"Listen, Roy," said Lonan, "while I don't really know Mister Bravo personally, we've been in some difficult spots together, and I think he's someone we can trust."

"I have to ask," Bravo turned his attention, "Lonan, just how did you get here? Last I heard, you'd walked out of the wilderness on Ansa and shipped off to your grandfather's home."

"My cousin, Josette," said Lonan, "sent killers to meet me."

Daestar raised an eyebrow in surprise at the accuracy of Bravo's previous guess about Lonan's circumstances.

"Wait," said Bravo, "I've seen her bodyguards. You're telling me that you survived an encounter with them?"

"Mostly by running away. The Kerks helped me escape."

Roy Kerk rotated his pilot's chair around to face Bravo and Daestar.

"We do a lot of that. Want to remind me why?"

"Thank you for saving us," said Daestar.

"Somehow, you knew exactly what I wanted to hear." Kirk turned back to the control console. "I think I've figured out a few things about our destination. Ever heard of a Lantern Star?"

"Isn't that two sun-like stars in a tight orbit?" Bravo asked. "Doesn't look like they're orbiting each other. Looks like they were merging together and something stopped them."

"My granddad called it a Lodestar," Roy brought up a satellite image. "He always used it to chart a path around that nebula. Those stars are so close together they look like a lantern. That's where your missus directed us."

"We're not married," said Daestar. "I mean, I'm married..."

"But not to me," Bravo clarified.

"I thought your last name was Bravo after you didn't give one earlier, but I knew you were married," said Roy. "Not because of all that blue jewelry you wear, but because you don't flirt. Out here in the deep nothing, lonely women get really flirty."

"And men get more aggressive," Daestar

whispered to Bravo.

"Look at how Pam keeps torturing poor Lonan," Roy added.

The words, "Again, not funny!" echoed from out of the main body of the ship.

"I'm going to finish getting the cannon ready." Lonan hurried off the bridge.

"Can't play Checkmate if you don't," Roy called after him.

Daestar noticed that Whip had been standing quietly, staring at the images of different regions of space that Roy had displayed on the monitors, rather than the milky white of hyper-light speed that surrounded them.

"Are you okay?"

"For an old man," he replied. "All my life I've wanted to be able to explore deep space. Now that I'm here, all I feel is empty."

"You've been through a shock, you'll adjust." She put a comforting hand his shoulder, even though her words were only a half-truth, knowing that nothing could make up for a stolen life.

A shimmy ran through the ship's gravity-enhanced floorboards as they dropped out of hyper-speed, and all the monitors switched to local view.

A wall of colorful gas loomed before them.

"I took us around to the opposite side of the star," said Roy, "so it'd look like we're approaching from Earth's side. Don't think we want to drop in on these people real sudden-like. We're going to come in at a crawl so they'll see us coming from a long way off."

A monitor focused on the Lantern Star slowly moved the star offscreen as a planet emerged from behind it.

"Want your first look at Corsairiana?" Roy popped the image on the forward view screen. "Think maybe we'll figure out a plan by the time we get there?"

"We do have an Ace card in Whip," said Daestar. "He looks exactly like the leader of the Artomiques."

"He does?" asked Roy. "So how does that help us?"

"We've recently learned that the Artomiques and pirates are working together," said Bravo.

"That's not a plan," Roy argued. "That's a

prayer. We need a plan."

"I'm not sure this is the sort of situation where you can make a plan," Bravo replied. "We're going to have to figure a way to get in without being boarded, and go from there."

"Well, we dumped all of our beer as a cover for sneaking you stowaways off that space station."

"Tell them the truth," said Daestar. "You're looking for equipment, and you're paying in gold. I think you have enough on board to bribe every pirate on that world."

Roy flipped on the ship's intercom system to make certain that Pam and Lonan heard his next words.

"We're going in on the greasy palm. Pull out a few bars of gold, just enough to get us planet-side."

"Are you sure that will work on pirates?" Bravo asked. "They've kept this world's location a secret. I doubt they'll be very welcoming of strangers."

"Ever met a pirate who didn't like gold?" Roy asked.

"No," Bravo replied. "And I never met one who wouldn't take everything you had."

"Me neither." Roy smiled to reassure Daestar. "And I've met a few. You've just got to keep them happy and confused at the same time. Since it's going to be a while before we get there, why don't you two go and relax? I'll let you know when we arrive."

Daestar followed Bravo off the bridge, hesitating a moment at Whip's side, but deciding at last to leave him to his reveries.

It had already been a long day, so both she and Bravo found a pair of unused crew bunks and laid down to rest. It seemed that she had just closed her eyes when Roy was calling "Miss Daestar" to the bridge.

Bravo was already there.

Corsairiana loomed large across the forward screen. It was a brownish world that looked like a partially peeled onion, having many terraces. There were high sections of land next to huge voids where oceans should have been. Very little water was seen anywhere, but the skies were filled with clouds. What made the moon-sized world unique was the bell-shaped world-engine erected at its southern pole, where the magnetic light show of the aurora australis danced about the metal structure taller than any mountain.

"Ever see anything like that?" Roy yawned when they entered, having been napping in the pilot's chair.

Bravo looked at the communications panel, then back to Daestar. She replied with a shrug of indifference. It was a sight familiar to them both.

"Here we go, folks." Roy reactivated the intercom. "They're sending a ship out to greet us. Pam, are you ready?"

"I'm always ready," came the reply, followed by a frustrated, "You know what I mean."

Roy smiled and winked at Bravo.

"I'm telling you," he said, "she's a pole dancer at heart, even if she doesn't realize it."

As the pirate ship drew closer, its gun ports began to glow, and it issued an all-band radio broadcast demanding a password.

"The Goodburger guys sent us," Roy replied back on all frequencies.

"Goodburger is an Earth world," Bravo whispered to Daestar, "where most interstellar beef is grown. I've always suspected that they had pirate affiliations."

There was a long pause before a reply came back.

"They would have given you a password."

"Oh," Roy replied, "they did. But it can't be broadcast over open frequencies. Ready your MCU."

The metal net of a Magnetic Capture Unit deployed on one side of the pirate ship.

"Got your target, Pam?" Roy called. "Fire."

Expecting them to launch a sneak attack, Daestar was surprised by two light, punting sounds. A pair of golden objects streaked across the void and landed directly in the center of the net, which quickly hauled them inside.

"That's the password, all right," an unshaven face popped up on one of the control console monitors.

Roy smiled back.

"Great. We're here to do some business."

"Follow us on down. But after we land, you're going to have to wait in your ship. Might be a while. There's a broadcast that's about to begin that everyone is supposed to be watching."

After the screen went empty, Roy turned to Daestar and Bravo with an equally blank look.

"What broadcast?"

"Only thing I know about," Bravo shrugged, "is the Earth-Wild Stars Conference that actually should be starting right about now. But I don't know why pirates would be watching it."

"Maybe to rile them up?" Roy hypothesized.

Following close to the pirate ship, the Gravedigger angled through the bigger ships parked in orbit and headed for the ground.

"What in the world is that?" Roy asked when the Godspeed came into view. "It looks like a giant space shark."

"That's the new Artomique dreadnought design," Bravo answered. "We seem to be following that beast around."

"That could be trouble for our Ace card," Daestar worried.

On an upper level of the terraced world was a hodgepodge of landing fields scattered across a thickly vegetated landscape that rose to meet them. At the very center of the terrace was a small complex of buildings, shining with thousands of lights. But there was no activity anywhere. There was no motion of vehicles on land or in the air, and no one could be seen moving about.

"Park next to us," was the last instruction given as the two crafts eased onto a mostly-open field next to a small building.

"Do you see that?" Roy pointed to the far side of the field, where a heavy-duty STS hauler was parked next to a shiny and complicated-looking piece of equipment, bigger than the building that the pirate crew hurried into.

"Doesn't look like it's been here long. I was wondering how the Gravedigger was going to haul that coupling back out into space, but it looks like all we have to do is commandeer that heavy hauler."

"Is that all?" asked Bravo. "As soon as those pirates see what you're up to, they'll blast you out of the sky before you even make low orbit."

"Got to distract them somehow," said Roy.

"Why don't you use that sexbot you've stored

below?" Whip asked as he joined them.

"No way," said Roy, "I've been saving her for a special occasion. And how do you even know about her? What are you, some dirty old man?"

"I was seventeen until days ago," Whip's response confused the captain, "and I recognize the packaging. It's an Artomique product and something we designed as an assassination device."

Roy's expression of defiance quickly changed to one of repulsion.

"Wait?" he said. "What? How does that work?"

"The human body contains 1,000 times the energy released by Earth's old Atomic bombs. Doesn't take much to cause a man to spontaneously combust. The Splendora model is equipped with serums that can trigger spontaneous combustion on a pre-selected timetable, injected by needles so tiny a victim doesn't even notice while they're otherwise occupied. So, if you time it right, the victim can also be used as the ultimate assassin, without ever knowing it. We call that time delay an $E=mc^2$ trigger. Turns mass into energy."

Daestar glared at Whip.

"Just how evil are you Artomiques?"

"Not me," Whip looked at Bully. "I was going to change everything when I took over. You were my inspiration, fighting the system to make a change for the better. That's what I wanted to do."

"You were never going to be allowed to take over," Daestar countered.

"I know that ... now."

"You can still make a difference," Bravo patted Whip's dejected shoulder. "You can still be an arbiter of change by helping us. Captain? About that sexbot?"

"Take her! Splendora is all yours."

Chapter Nine:
Pam, the Erotic Pole Dancer

When the lounge door opened, all the air in the room seemed to vanish and everyone inside gasped.

"Oh, my lord, lord, lord!" one man stuttered as every jaw in the room dropped.

Standing in the doorway with bronzed skin shining like a beacon against the darkness of the night outside was the most physically perfect and beautiful woman that any of the men present had ever seen, completely naked and striking a provocative pose. Chairs screeched across the room as half a dozen pirates immediately rose, some of them spilling their beverages. Shattering glass was the only sound as all the women cocked their heads sideways, glanced at each other, and nodded begrudgingly. The image projected on the far wall that had held the room's complete focus a moment before, now went unnoticed.

"I brought you boys a present," Whip announced as he walked the Spendora into the room, guiding the limited intelligence of its operating system with a hand on her shoulder. When she saw a raised section of flooring that featured a metal pole in the center, her programming took over. She began to strut, dance, and tease as she approached the stage with steps so light that she seemed to float across the floor. No one in the room cared that she never spoke.

"I didn't think that was humanly possible," one clueless man remarked when the Splendora stood sideways on the pole. Because of the lightness of her polymer skeleton, she was able to balance with a foot on either side of the pole. She began to rotate slowly around like a propeller blade, flirting with every man and woman she passed.

"Meet Pam!" Whip took a step back in the direction of the door.

"What?" A woman's voice shrieked into his earpiece.

"Only real name I could think of," he whispered with a hand covering a fake clearing of the throat.

The largest and most heavily tattooed man in the room had stayed in his seat, situated directly between Whip and the exit. Slowly setting his beer down, the pirate gave a shake of the head to clear the hair blocking his eyes, which were focused on Whip instead of the dancer. When the pirate stood, Whip could see the injector knife hanging at his side. Outlawed across the stars, those blades expelled highly pressurized CO_2 into a victim, instantly freezing their internal organs. The size of the knife hilt determined how many wounds they could inflict, although once per victim was usually as fatal as it was painful. This pirate's knife and hilt were the size of a machete.

"Sir?" the pirate asked with a demeanor of respect. "Shouldn't you be at Red Queen's citadel?" He gave a confused glance at the wall image filled with differently dressed men who gathered in a large amphitheater room with many levels of seating. "She said this was your party. I've got a grav-skipper sitting right outside."

"Sure," Whip squeaked and coughed to recover a voice that he was not yet acclimated to. "Listen, I've got a crew working on a special assignment outside. Make sure no one interrupts them."

"Everyone, stay put—hear me?" the pirate shouted, and received no response. He turned back to Whip. "I don't think they'll be interrupting anyone for a few hours. Doubt they'll be watching any shows, either." He smiled at another of the artificial Pam's acrobatic moves and turned his head sideways to keep his eyes level with hers.

"Tell them I'm going with you," Daestar's voice spoke next in Whip's ear, drawing an argument from Bravo, who at first protested and then wanted to come along. She shut that down with, "Roy and Pam need your help. I have to circulate around to try and find my children. Whip, when we get started, tell the pilot to fly low and circle all the buildings. Tell him you're doing an inspection."

When Whip stepped outside, he caught a glimpse of Bravo slipping out of sight around the corner of the building. Daestar was waiting there, putting on a show of impatience and indifference for the pirate, who never noticed Bravo.

"She's real," Whip put an arm out to stop the pirate's attempt at a physical inspection, "and she's coming with us."

The pirate did not reply, his gaze drifting to the massive power coupling that sat at the far end of the landing zone, balanced on its thick center section and tilted to one of the matching smaller sides, where transport cables still hung. When he looked away, he saw the Gravedigger.

"We should put some guards on that ship."

"What's your name?" Whip asked.

"Takeshak. Slane Takeshak."

"Well, Slane, I'll be mentioning your name to the Red Queen when I see her. But first I have to get there."

Slane understood Whip's implication and led the way to a small, four-person gravity-skipper parked by the corner of the building—right next to where Bravo had just disappeared. But Bravo had apparently kept moving and was nowhere to be seen when they boarded the craft.

"Take me on a tour," Whip instructed as the open-air craft rose on an anti-gravity pulse. The ride was a new experience for Whip. Gravity-skippers had replaced most motorized and wheeled vehicles on Earth, but Whip had never been allowed to ride one. Being highly maneuverable and capable of tackling almost any terrain other than vertical, they were the leading cause of accidental deaths.

"Don't smile," Daestar whispered as Slane began working in a circular pattern in the direction of a red citadel that towered over the terraces. There was a delay before Whip realized that her mouth had never moved.

Gazing down at the passing buildings, Daestar leaned against the open-air window railing, the wind whipping her long, blond hair all about.

The lights below were all on, but the walkways were empty.

Some of the terraces were devoid of life, with habitations rarely built on the top levels. Every piece of undeveloped ground seemed to be connected by riotous plant growth that sent long, hanging vines down to connect with the levels below.

Whip was beginning to understand just how uniquely suited gravity-skippers were for the uneven terrain of Corsairiana. The craft moved agilely up and down, sometimes skimming beneath a jutting ledge not overgrown by a canopy of dark avocado green. When they passed too low above one tumble of green, a cloud of bulbous, nearly transparent balls of flesh were bounced up into the air by the skipper's antigravity pulse. These basketball-sized creatures had tiny tendrils hanging from their bottom and large, elephant-like ears that flapped to control their movement as they either slowly dropped back to the brush or caught a breeze and floated away. Two shiny, unblinking, saucer-shaped eyes reflected the starlight.

"Windsquid," Whip nudged Daestar and nodded in the direction of the cloud of flesh bubbles that began to spread in all directions.

"Would your father notice them?" Once again Daestar's words echoed in his head without any movement of her lips.

Slane seemed a little confused about what his passengers might be doing behind his back and, to be discreet, activated a hologram on the skipper's control console to provide a distraction.

The same images that Whip had seen back in the lounge popped up. It caught Daestar's attention when she seemed to recognize the man addressing the gathered representatives from across the Wild Stars and the Earth's scattered colonies. The voice emanating from the hologram drowned out the voices of Bravo and the Kerks in Whip's ear, as they labored to reconnect the cables hanging from the massive power coupling to the heavy-duty hauler. Their voices faded as the distance between them widened.

"The Wild Stars have been gone from this region for some time." Standing at the podium on the amphitheater stage, Erlik began to address the attendees, who quieted as they settled into their assigned seating.

"When Earth made their second migration into the stars, there were constant conflicts of authority over the outer colonies. United Nations Interstellar Peacekeepers were woefully outnumbered and out-armed by the I.C.—Interstellar Conglomerate—and other Global Conglomerates intent on becoming Stellar Conglomerates. They financed much of the expense of exploration and shared none of the profits. Some, such as the Terraformers and Artomiques, still operate today and wield more power than many worlds combined."

Slane gave a sideways glance to Whip, who did his best to show no reaction. All his life, Whip had been trained in the ways of asserting command, and even though the training had only been a show in preparation for when his father took over his body,

it served him well as he nodded for the pirate to keep his eyes straight ahead.

"The outer colonies formed their own alliances of families, much like the early pioneers of the American West."

The pirate began smiling as Erlik continued.

"Pirates were everywhere. And every pirate belonged to a certain ship or clan. There are even stories of the descendants of the Knights Templar, who have long waited for the Wild Stars' return."

Erlik paused a moment, looking around the room.

"Now, that wait has ended. We're back. We're not aliens from another world. The peoples of the Wild Stars all came from Earth during an earlier migration, some 75,000 years ago. We are one family. And we're gathered here today to join as one."

Slane shook his head as they neared the red citadel.

Daestar also shook her head, but in apparent frustration as she signaled Whip by cutting her eyes back in the direction they had come.

But before Whip could tell Slane to reverse course, Daestar grabbed his arm, her attention suddenly turned to a landing pad near the top of the citadel tower.

"Take us up," Whip instructed.

On the hologram, Erlik introduced a speaker who represented colonies in the Terran asteroid belt. She smiled politely as she worked her way to the podium, thanked the host, and began to elaborate on the colonial history and to justify Roider rage with Earth.

As Slane guided the skipper to one edge of the citadel, Whip was intrigued by its construction. A spiral ornamental design rose from the ground and looped upward around the building like a coiled snake that reached to the balconies at the very top. But as they drew closer, he could see that these were actually several lines of protrusions embedded within the outer shell. Too far apart for a human to traverse, they provided the perfect avenue for a skipper to scale the otherwise vertical tower. There were no other breaks anywhere else on the citadel's exterior—no windows nor even a ground floor entrance. The only access was at the very top, which, as they neared, the lower rows of protrusions stopped at lower balconies, all of which were open to the air. Slane took the high course that led to the very top.

The skipper bypassed a smaller, adjacent balcony filled with other vehicles that included shuttles and hovercraft and proceeded to the main balcony that still harbored a handful of open spaces.

Through the doorways, they saw an expansive room that encompassed the entire width of the tower's top. It was filled with scantily clad women mixing with lower-caste diplomats conversing with flamboyantly dressed pirates. Whip noticed that no women of power were apparent, but knew this was misleading. Daestar mentally whispered to him about how the Five-Thousand Fingered Hand always hid their presence.

"I was wrong," Daestar gripped his arm, pulling him back toward the skipper for a moment before releasing him. Then her voice grew softer and more distant in his mind. "This place looks like fun. Go—enjoy yourself."

When a trio of beautiful women approached and reached for his hands, pulling him into the cavernous room where a large hologram presented the Ansa broadcast, Whip did not resist.

The women pulled him to one side and immediately began plying him with strong drinks that made his head spin. Then they led him willingly to a thickly cushioned chair at the bottom of the sunken floor in the center of the room, right next to the holographic display. Then the shortest woman waved the others away.

Pushing him back into the cushions, she promptly sat on his lap and began curling a finger around one of his ears while she leaned in and inserted her tongue into the other. It was a sensation Whip had never experienced before.

"My name is Candy," she whispered. "April Candy."

Chapter Ten:
The Fall of the Wild Stars Begins

Too late, Daestar realized that the telepathic presence she had sensed was not that of her children. Only when they arrived at the top of the tower did the presence fully manifest itself as being something far more powerful than anything that her two children could generate.

Daestar tried to warn Whip and reached for his arm, but Slane quickly moved to break that grip and pulled her away, clamping a hand across her mouth.

Another psychic voice drowned her own as it spoke into Whip's mind, while three young women pulled him blithely into the heart of the Red Citadel. Only when he was lost to sight did Slane release her.

Spinning, Daestar confronted the telepath who had been lurking on her blind side from the moment she arrived.

"Whip!" Daestar called out audibly.

"Oh, he can't hear you," said the red-headed woman dressed in a brightly sequined red dress, framed by a flowing floor-length cape that had a red underside and black exterior. "I've given him some candy to distract him."

"Who are you?" Daestar demanded.

"Please," chided the woman, "you know who I am."

Daestar held up the index finger of her right hand.

"You're the finger that points all the other fingers of the Five-Thousand-Fingered Hand. You're also a pirate leader called the Red Queen. Your mark is a red skull atop a pair of crossed bones. I heard you were dead."

The Red Queen smiled, walking seemingly absent-mindedly in a circle around Daestar, but all the while, both women were engaged in furious psychic assaults on each other. If the battle of their minds were visible to the unsuspecting bystanders, they would have seen giant walls of crystal being shattered by pointed flames of mental fire, layer after layer, while shards of crystal and sparks of fire exploded from the center of their conflict in every direction.

"I heard the same about you," the Red Queen replied with a calm that belied her outpouring of mental energy. "Daestar of Vahn. Two hundred years ago, you and your sister were a pair of fingers on our Hand. Twins always make the most powerful telepaths. We were surprised to learn that you'd escaped in the company of the Ancient Warrior's last

surviving son. Well done. But you never followed through on the Hand's mandate. You infiltrated the immortals, but you did nothing to destroy them. If anything, you helped them. Why? Another finger had already started the work. You were in a position to finish it."

"The Immortals are not the evil beings I was told they were," Daestar replied.

"Ah..." said the Red Queen, "but you did the work. I can see a Book of Circles in your mind. You absorbed the experiences of those you encountered along with the Immortal Erlik and Ancient Warrior... even his daughter... and assembled them into a visual narrative of collected memories. Why did you not share this Book? If you had, Erlik's daughter, Akara, would have become part of our Hand. Her grandmother was one of our Fingers, so Akara was born to be one of our thousands."

"You mentioned my sister." Daestar realized she was losing the fight by how easily the Red Queen had seen inside her head. But she refused to quit. "She was off-world when Vahn was destroyed. Whatever happened to her?"

"She wasn't with us when the Wild Stars departed for the horseshoe galaxy. What was a journey of only a couple of decades for us was a couple of hundred Earth years in this galaxy. Your sister was probably lost in the stars on some ugly world after your home was destroyed, and died a tragic and horrible death—all alone—so sad."

Daestar knew she was being baited emotionally and was surprised when the Red Queen suddenly abated in her attack.

"The show is just starting to get interesting." The Red Queen motioned Daestar inside and to a seat on the outer, raised perimeter of the room that circled the sunken floor with a holographic emitter in the center.

Slane followed them, hovering close by.

Seated in a chair close to the display, Daestar located Whip and gave a psychic call for help. But her message was either blocked by the Red Queen, or he was oblivious to her presence as his face was locked in a passionate kiss with a beautiful young woman not even half his body's age.

Daestar begrudgingly turned her attention to the hologram, using the moment's respite to plan an escape.

On the display, each of the colonial and planetary representatives speaking in the Council Chambers on Ansa had been taking turns lamenting their poor relationships with Earth and were excited about the prospect of having an ally against them. Erlik held up his hand and stood before the next speaker was called.

"My friends," he said, "we're not here to create an alliance against Earth. In fact, it's my hope that Earth will become a fast friend to all who live in the Wild Stars. Former President Bully Bravo will be arriving here soon to speak on this matter. In the meantime, I want to introduce you to a man who represents two worlds, both Earth and the world many of you call Akara's world."

The hologram shifted focus to Erlik's daughter, Akara, who immediately stood and walked for the exit, with Mack following close behind with an arm wrapped around the shoulder of his hesitant daughter, Risky's wife Atlanta, who looked to be the same age as her parents. Atlanta resisted passing through the doorway, and Akara also seemed unsure of her own reactions as she too paused and listened to Erlik's next words.

"Earthers once called this world Magus IV. The Wild Stars have always called it Miri. So, I guess it's appropriate that our next speaker also has multiple names. On Earth, he's known as Risky Bravo, President Bravo's brother. On Miri, we call him Tomas Shawnee, father of Bully Shawnee."

There was a smattering of confused applause and a rumbling of his son's many heroic nicknames as Risky stood and walked to the podium, which he clutched for support against shaky legs.

"Out here in the vastness of the deep cold," Risky's voice was as shaky as his legs at first, but smoothed out, "every outpost of humanity knows just how much they have to rely only on themselves. Against threats such as the wolf-like Brothan, it's good to have friends, but on Miri, the Brothan remain. True, their Brotan God is dead, and, no longer being reinforced by new recruits, they have been beaten back to isolated pockets and gone feral. But another old enemy is now trying to reinsert themselves into our world—one we'd hoped was gone forever—an enemy everyone here is familiar with—the Black-Eyes of Earth."

Erlik could be seen shifting uncomfortably in his seat as a roar of agreement swept the room. He looked at the empty chair where Admiral Bryce would normally have sat.

Daestar figured that Bryce's absence was probably deliberate, knowing that Erlik had reduced the Earth's presence at this stage of the conference, where grievances would be aired. What surprised her was the agitated demeanor of the normally collected Risky Bravo. He was not behaving as she would have expected. Having recently been reborn in a clone body, he would be expected to need a period of adjustment, but still, Daestar worried for him.

"The population of that blue marble I once called home thinks only of themselves and their needs," Risky continued. "They have attempted to strip Miri once before of her mineral and natural resources. When they thought Miri faced imminent doom, they abandoned us. Now that we've survived, they're coming back."

Risky turned and looked at Erlik.

"I'll give credit to my brother, President Bully Bravo. During his time in office, he managed to hold that tide back. But, as someone else once said, Earthmen are like a plague of locusts—locusts with the appetites of great white sharks—and they look at all the scattered outposts of humanity as their servants. They demand what we have, and want control over us and to tell us how we're going to live in order to guarantee their deliveries."

He paused for a moment while the murmur of agreement grew louder. Then Risky reached into a pocket and pulled out the Icarus stone. Light glistened on its bands of gold when he held it up for all to see.

"This little stone is a deed of ownership in the Wild Stars. It's the title to a planet—this one is for Earth."

Risky began tossing the stone in the air and catching it.

"It is very light, which is about how much weight it carries with me. I do not recognize that a world, be it Earth, Miri, or any of your worlds or outposts, can be owned by anyone other than its occupants."

A jubilant roar silenced Risky for a moment.

"This," he continued to toss the stone, ever higher, "this is what I think about titles of ownership!"

He caught the falling stone and wheeled his arm in a roundhouse circle, throwing it to the floor as hard as he could.

The moment the stone struck, every monitor in the Red Citadel went blank except the holograph in the center of the room. It showed what had happened as it displayed a freeze-frame of the last nano-second of the broadcast. From the spot of the stone's impact, a shock wave spread out and across the room in every direction, instantly vaporizing Risky, Erlik, and all those nearest to it. The freeze-frame showed the anguish of those being torn apart by the edge of the blast and the horror of those it was about to strike.

The image then fluttered and disappeared, to be replaced with a distant view of the capital city of Ansa, where a billowing cloud of smoke rose from the burning center of the city. When the passionless voice of a limited intelligence reporter droid reported the facts already known by every viewer, its words were damning.

"The explosion was apparently caused by Risky Bravo, once considered by Earth to be a terrorist and later exonerated by his brother, President Bravo. Questions are now being asked if this original charge of terrorism, which followed the massive explosions all across the Prairie Bay region of Mars, might not have been justified. All attempts to contact former President Bravo have failed, as his current location is unknown. Attempts are being made at this moment to contact former Mars Supreme Commander Cinceno for comment. The former Mars Commander was court-martialed by President Bravo. Reports are already coming in that President Perez is now reviewing the legality of that action. More on all these stories when new details become available."

Daestar sat stunned, having just watched the love of her life simply blink out of existence before her eyes. She had been physically and mentally staggered.

"We've done it!" the Red Queen gloated. "The Five-Thousand Fingered Hand will finally rid our galaxy of the scourge of immortal manipulators. Only one more to go."

Daestar heard the words, but her mind was still reeling from the devastation of what she had seen. She was barely able to manage a single psychic call for help, that she was certain would go unheeded.

The Red Queen saw her opportunity and took it.

"Have you ever heard of a psychic knife?" she whispered and formed her right hand into a fist, which she then slammed into the back of Daestar's head.

Daestar screamed and fell forward, all of her psychic barriers shattered as the Red Queen cut deep into her mind and ravaged about like sprayed acid.

When Daestar fell limp to the floor, her eyes were barely cognizant of what was happening. The Red Queen towered triumphantly over her and then turned away.

"Takeshak," she summoned the pirate, "take this refuse away from here—away from me. Have some fun and then dispose of what's left."

With a leering smile, Slane greedily scooped Daestar up off the floor with much inappropriate touching that foretold of his intentions.

He carried her back to his skipper and hurriedly launched off the balcony into open air and free-fell in a quick descent, whooping and hollering the whole way down.

Chapter Eleven:
A Taste of April Candy

When April Candy ran her tongue across his cheek, Whip responded likewise and found the taste of this young woman to be more intoxicating than any of the liquid concoctions he had just experienced for the very first time.

All of his life, he had been sequestered away by his advisors. He had seen and encountered many

beautiful women and young girls, but had always been blocked from physical contact.

"When you're old enough to run the corporation," he was told, "then you'll be old enough to choose a lover. The wrong woman can not only lie and mislead you, she can leave you with biological *gifts* that you don't want."

Whip had always wondered how he was supposed to gain that knowledge without any actual experience, but now understood that his body was being kept clean until it could be taken away. Long had he fantasized what actual contact would be like, stimulated by thoughts of a Splendora companion. Finding himself in the company of the real thing, thoughts of a Splendora no long stirred his desires. At first, he blamed the body he had been imprisoned inside. Now, the enthusiastic young woman named April had shown him that his body was still indeed capable of arousal.

April's raven-black hair hung in his face as she planted a series of wet kisses across his lips, probing his tongue with hers, and then proceeded to kiss his neck. Her olive-tan skin was flawless and unblemished, and carried an aroma that was both sweet and musky.

Whip took a deep breath through his nose, and something seemed to snap inside his mind. He saw a phantom image of what looked like a crystal shell forming in the air around him. It vanished as quickly as it appeared.

"I'll let you watch the show," April whispered as she snuggled so close that Whip thought their two bodies were merging into one, "for now."

Whip could have cared less about what was happening on the holo-display, until he saw the Icarus stone being tossed up and down in Risky's hands.

"Is he a fool?" Whip recoiled when the stone was slammed into the floor and everyone in the display was rent to shreds. "It was a bomb?"

Up until this moment, Whip had thought it was his idea to hand the Icarus stone to Risky. But now he began to remember how Genghis and Georgian insisted that the stone be given to an Earthman, and repeatedly suggested that it should be Risky. Whip realized that he had been used as a time-delayed assassin.

Something inside his head clicked, and the walls of crystal returned. Instinctively, he knew that he was seeing a mental manifestation of his mind trying to protect itself. As soon as that thought occurred, the soft voice of Daestar repeatedly urging him to enjoy himself abruptly disappeared. It was replaced by her voice crying for help.

Whip tried to stand, but his new body was not capable of the things his old one had been, and he was pinned in the chair by Candy's weight. Unwilling to accept his new limitations, Whip forced himself to rise to a standing position, holding the giggling girl in his arms. Despite the fact that she was small and light, he still struggled with her weight and his balance.

Too late, he caught sight of a limp Daestar being carried away in a much more undignified manner by Slane Takeshak, who tossed her into the back of his skipper. Whip tried to follow but lost his balance and stumbled sideways on the steps.

Before he fell completely, April Candy gently slipped from his arms, took his hand, and led Whip toward the smaller balcony. He went willingly and rushed to the platform's edge. Far below, he saw Slane's skipper falling nearly to the ground, where its anti-gravity repulsors finally caught something to bounce off from. With several large hops that became successively shallower, the skipper bounded away in the direction of where the Gravedigger had landed.

"Let's you and I take one," April urged and pulled him in the direction of another skipper. "Find someplace to be alone."

As Whip started the repulsor motor and prepared to launch, April's giggles turned into a gasp.

The Red Queen was marching straight toward them, hand-signaling for every pirate she passed to fall in line behind her.

"Where do you think you're going?" The demanding tone of her voice made April shiver.

Inside his head, Whip heard even more words from the Red Queen.

"How are you doing this? That brain was trained

in psychic defense, but your mind isn't. You can't resist me."

Whip proved her wrong as he opened the throttle and shot the skimmer out into the air, leaving his stomach behind as the rapid fall disorientated him for a moment.

April screamed the whole way down.

Before they hit the ground, Whip had the skipper under full control, and they bounced away, following Slane and Daestar.

"What are you doing?" April's voice was filled with desperation and fear as she watched the Red Citadel recede behind them. "The Red Queen told me that you two were allies—that you're the most powerful man on Earth. She's going to think that I did something to you!"

"Why would she think that?" asked Whip, relieved when his earbud finally began to catch whispers of conversations from the Gravedigger's crew.

"Because of who I am," April answered. "Because of my parents."

Whip wanted to ask her to explain more, but by then the voices in his ear became louder and clearer.

"Gravedigger," he called, to the confusion of April. He tapped his ear when he continued. "Can you hear me?"

"We can," Bully Bravo's voice answered.

"Do you know what happened?" Whip asked. "Pam, were you watching the broadcast on the ship?"

"We've been kind of busy?" was her reply.

"Never mind," said Whip. "Right now, you need to get out of here as fast as you can. This whole place is about to erupt in a celebration. Hopefully, you can slip away in the confusion."

"What are you talking about?" asked Bravo. "Where's Daestar? Are you in one of those skippers headed our way?"

"I'm in the second one," Whip replied. "Daestar has been taken prisoner by the pirate I met earlier. I'm going to get her back."

"I saw that pirate," Bravo replied, "and you're not going to be able to stop him from doing anything he wants. Damn!"

Bravo's curse was a reaction to Slane Takeshak skipping once off the terrace where the Gravedigger was parked and then dropping down to another terrace below.

"Don't worry about me," Whip argued back. "Just get those ships in the air before it's too late. Daestar and I will find another way off this world."

"No," said April, "you won't. And if any of those ships launch, they'll be shot down. It's a trap—that you set. Don't you remember?"

"Negative on that launch," Whip called back. "Apparently, the pirates are waiting for something like this. Get back to the Gravedigger and hunker down. Act like you never left."

There was an argument about that plan between Pam and Roy, who wanted to launch anyway. Bravo's voice silenced them.

"Everyone! Listen to me. Roy, you and Lonan get back to the Gravedigger. No arguments! I'm going after Daestar."

"I'm going to get her back," Whip reiterated his intention and double-tapped his ear to silence Bravo's protests.

"You're going after Slane Takeshak?" April asked breathlessly as the skipper bounced off the terrace and followed the other one down to the next level below, scattering a cloud of wind-squid as they passed through. "You're going to die, and you're going to get me killed, too! Can't you see the sky? It's going to rain soon?"

"So?" Whip asked, but there was no time for her to answer when their skipper landed right next to where a startled Slane had just parked his. Aimed downward, the skipper's ground lights could only produce a slight luminescence.

"You?" the pirate called out incredulously and instinctively looked in the direction of the Red Citadel, as if looking for some sort of instruction.

"The woman," Whip demanded in his most authoritarian voice, "give her to me. Now!"

"You aren't him, not anymore," said Slane as he stepped out of his skipper and pulled his injector knife. "The Red Queen told me so. The only thing I'm giving you is a quick and ugly death."

There came a crack of thunder as clouds covered

the stars with a black blanket, and all the wind-squid turned at once and began flapping for shelter.

Slane was also distracted by the thunder, as he hesitated and held the palm of his hand up. Detecting no rain, he gave an evil smile that looked even more sinister with the defused ground lights from the skippers distorting the shadows on his face.

"Get us out of here," April begged and reached for the controls. Whip blocked her and shook his head. He had been well trained in the martial arts, and hoped that the body he now inhabited had maintained some semblance of training. Then he remembered how he had struggled to lift April, and began to reconsider his actions. But it was too late for reason to overrule the impulse of adrenalin-driven decisions.

Slane stepped into the back of Whip's skipper, waving his injector blade and tossing it from one hand to the other and back again several times.

"Hello, little Candy," Slane said to April. "When I'm done with him, and done with her," he nodded back to his skipper, "then you and me are going to have fun for a long, long time."

April shuddered.

"Takeshak," she asked, "Why are you threatening Mister Achilles? What do you mean... that he's not him anymore?"

"He's a Hister," said Slane, "But he's not Achilles. Not the real one."

Whip stepped in front of her, bent his knees, and held his arms out, bringing them slowly together in front of him as he tried to form his hands and fingers for combat, but they did not completely bend the way he wanted them too.

"He's right," said Whip. "I'm not my father."

"Wow," April gasped, "either one of you looks really old, or one of you looks really young, or both!"

Slane laughed aloud and brought his knife-arm back as he prepared to thrust and lunge forward. Then a loud rustling in the vines hanging from the terrace above distracted him.

Stepping back out of the skipper to get a better view of what was happening above him, Slane seemed surprised when someone else joined them, sliding down the vines like a climber on a rope.

"Whoever you are," Slane shouted to the interloper whose face was hidden in the dark, "start climbing back up. This is my party."

Then Slane heard the noise of another person climbing down to join them, albeit in a much slower and more deliberate manner.

"What is this?" the pirate demanded.

Bully Bravo wasted neither his time nor his breath as he lunged forward in an all-out assault on the pirate. His punches to Slane's face and midsection all landed with the slap of a meat cleaver breaking flesh and bone, and he closed to grappling distance—inside the reach of Slane's massive blade. But the pirate was a big man, and while staggered by Bravo's blows, he did not go down. Instead, Slane began to grapple back, positioning himself to strike with his knife.

Before Slane could deal a deathblow, April had run from the skipper and grabbed his arm, holding it back. Whip had moved at the same time that she had, and quickly joined her in the effort.

Like a big cat being annoyed by kittens, Slane grabbed Bravo by the neck and extended his arm so that the former President could not land any more blows as he choked to death. The pirate waved his other arm about in a futile attempt to dislodge Whip and April, and finally simply lifted them up until their feet no longer touched the ground.

Slane let out a grunting laugh at the ridiculousness of the fight and prepared to stab Bravo with his blade. Then a flash of recognition changed his snarl into a look of excitement.

"You're Bully Bravo. I get to kill me a President!"

That was when the other climber descending from above decided to jump the final distance and landed on the pirate's back with force enough to drive him to the ground. April pulled his fingers out of joint one at a time, finally causing him to drop the knife.

Having lost all his leverage and his grip on Bravo, Slane struggled just to rise back to his knees. But Bravo was already on his back and had his arms locked about the pirate's neck with a lethal sleeper hold. With all blood to his brain stopped, Slane started to slump to the ground. Then he found a sudden surge of energy and jolted to his feet, dislodging everyone clinging to him.

Bravo hit the ground and bounced right back up, lunging with a shoulder into Slane's mid-section and driving him to the very edge of the narrow terrace, at a spot where little vegetation grew.

The pair then circled about, each man knocking the other's hands away before they could gain a grip. Slane grimaced as he snapped his dislocated fingers back into place, and then lunged forward in another attempt to seize Bravo by the neck. But the former President pivoted around so that Slane found himself teetering on the terrace's crumbling edge until his weight sent him over. Slane managed to break his fall as he found a grip on a half-buried rock and clung tightly.

Whip rushed to the terrace's edge, and saw the panic that filled the pirate's eyes. He called back to April and Lonan to use the pirate's fallen knife to cut away a vine to use as a rope.

Bravo neither helped nor interfered as Whip lowered the vine down to the pirate but stood ready with clenched fists. He looked around, as if searching for something that he could not find.

Slane grabbed the dangling vine and began climbing up. With each hand pull to safety, Whip watched the pirate's expression change from fear back to hate. As Slane neared the top, he reached with one hand and pulled another knife.

Whip let go of the vine, watching the pirate's look of horror return as he fell backwards and disappeared into the darkness below.

"That was cruel," said Lonan.

"No," said April. "It wasn't."

Bravo patted Whip on the shoulder as everyone sagged with their hands on their knees, the dilated pupils of their eyes slowly shrinking back to normal as the adrenalin stopped pumping through their veins.

"Why didn't you stop me?" Whip asked.

"It was a lesson you had to learn." Bravo looked at April. "Who's your new friend?"

"Thanks," Whip said first to April, and then repeated his appreciation to Bravo and Lonan Mcguffin.

"I thought I told you to get to the Gravedigger?"

Bravo admonished Lonan.

"You stood by me through many dangers on Ansa," Lonan replied. "And still I ran away every time. I'm not that frightened boy anymore, and I'm tired of always running away. I ran away from my cousin. I'm not going to run anymore."

"Hi, I'm Candy," April said to Lonan as she extended her hand in greeting. Whip could tell that she had already forgotten him completely, as she became instantly infatuated by the handsome young man who was so much closer to her own age.

"Candy, is it?" said Bravo. "I want to thank you, too. I might be dead now, if not for you."

"April Candy," she replied with an absent-minded tone, never breaking eye contact with Lonan. Then a drop of rain landed on her arm, and she jumped, startled. "It's about to rain. We've got to get to shelter!"

"Why?" Whip asked. "A little rain won't hurt us."

"Maybe the rain won't," April replied, "but the things that hunt in the rain *will*."

"See that?" Bravo pointed Whip to the fluttering cloud of wind-squid, futilely trying to work their way to shelter as they began being battered to the ground by an ever increased volume of rain. "I've seen them on other planets. Wherever they are, there are predators who only come out in the rain, hunting them when they can't fly."

The clouds cracked open with a fresh barrage of thunder and lightning, releasing a torrent of rain that drove every wind-squid still airborne straight to the ground, many of them landing nearby where they flopped about in a frantic panic.

As everyone hurried for the shelter of the skippers, Bravo paused to pick up Slane's injector knife where April had dropped it.

"We all need to get into the same one," April urged when the group began to split into the different skippers.

Whip wiped the rain from his face as he kneeled over the fallen Daestar, lifting her up to a sitting position. He was surprised when her eyes showed recognition, but she neither spoke audibly nor in his head.

"What's wrong with her?" Bravo asked as he stepped into the skipper's shelter, shaking off the rain like a wet dog.

"I've seen this before," said April. "The Red Queen calls it a psychic knife attack."

"Will she get better?" Whip asked.

April shook her head and slumped her shoulders in ignorance.

Then the skipper was jolted by a large body brushing against it. Everyone looked to see a mass of nightmarish shapes, defined only by the reflection of the skipper's ground lights reflecting off the rain splattering across their backs, crawling up over the edge of the terrace.

Chapter Twelve:
The Darklaw Legacy

A flash of lightning revealed the creatures approaching the skipper. Their bulbous, white bodies were covered with patchy strands of long, purple hair. They had stalklike arms and yellow pincers with blood-red cutting edges in place of their forearms, and no heads. A single, massive eye peered out from the center of their bodies, with red spokes radiating out from around it.

"Most colonists call them Peppermints," Bravo whispered, "because of the red and white markings around their eye. Everyone get down on the floor."

As the creatures moved past, they became flatulent, loudly emitting a stench that not even the rain could not knock down.

"Hold your breath as long as you can," Bravo whispered when a pincher reached through one of the skipper's windows, its claws clacking ominously while searching briefly about before withdrawing.

"The stench," April replied in a voice too loud, "it's so awful."

"Hold on," Bravo urged. "They do that to scare off other predators. They're almost gassed out."

Whip peered over the edge of a window when another series of lightning flashes revealed the Peppermints searching out the wind-squid who had been stranded across the terrace, squatting over them and then waddling away on their clumsy hind legs that, being attached to the sides of their bodies,

were better suited for climbing. Nothing was left behind.

The next flash of lightning showed a barren terrace, empty of both Peppermints and fallen wind-squid.

Whip breathed a sigh of relief.

"They're gone," he announced as the rain simultaneously relented.

As the storm clouds passed and revealed the twinkling of stars once more, fireworks began to filling the sky from the direction of the Red Citadel, and a multitude of craft began to fill the air.

Bully Bravo looked at April.

"Think we can slip past them to rejoin our friends?"

"Only a fool would go back up there," April replied. "Our only hope is to go down to the lowest levels."

"What's down there?" Lonan asked.

"My family," April leaned into Lonan, with her face upturned to his.

Bravo tapped his earbud.

"Roy? Pam? Stay put. We're going to hide until the show dies down. No! Don't try to take off."

Whip heard the other side of the conversation from his earbud.

"You people are the ones who left," said Roy. "Our deal was to get you to Corsairiana. Not to stick around like a taxi with the meter running. If you're not back by the time we lift off, then you're staying."

"What about Lonan?" Bravo asked. "He's with us."

"What?" Pam exclaimed so loudly that Whip winced in pain. She then proceeded to inform Roy that they were not going anywhere until Lonan returned.

"Listen," Bravo interjected into the ensuing argument. "If you wait, you're going to have a better chance to escape later. Right now, you'll be the only ship lifting off, and you'll get all the attention from those big cruisers in orbit. Regardless of whether we make it back or not, stay on the ground until there's a distraction that you can use to your advantage."

"What kind of distraction?" Roy asked.

"One you'll recognize when it happens," Bravo

replied. "When it does, you should be able to sail away with no trouble. We'll try to find our way back to you before that. I estimate that we have until daybreak."

Bravo double-tapped his ear to end the conversation. He then took the controls of the skipper and looked at April.

"Okay, little lady, show me where we can hide for a few hours."

With the skipper's ground lighting set to its dimmest setting, the vehicle slowly wound its way from one terrace down to the next. The planet's surface erosion made the Badlands of the North American Dakotas look mild, with whole sections carved out of every side of the major pinnacles of rock and soil that had been solidified by ground vegetation. Terrace ridges of varying heights and thicknesses filled the major gaps between them with green islands in the air.

"What were you talking about earlier?" asked Bravo. "The only broadcast I know about that might be of any interest is the Ansa conference."

Whip looked at Daestar, leaned up against a wall, nodding and rolling her head with the movement of the skipper. It seemed to him that she nodded yes, so he proceeded to tell Bravo about what he had seen at the Red Citadel.

Hearing the news about the explosion, Bravo stopped their descent and parked the skipper on a narrow terrace along a ridge that ran all the way to Red Citadel, barely visible in the mist raised by the recent rain.

Whip was astonished at how well the former president was processing the news about the death of his brother. There were no tears, but Bravo's face did harden and his jaw muscles flexed from the grinding of his molars.

"Any chance some of them might have escaped?" Bravo asked.

"It happened like..." Whip snapped his fingers, "that. It was instantaneous. But that's not the worst of it."

Bravo's expression was incredulous.

"The news reports are being slanted to blame you because..."

"Because Risky was my brother." Bravo finished the sentence.

"And there's that thing that happened on Mars."

"Risky saved those people," Bravo snapped back, "by getting that Marzanti trident off the planet."

"I don't think most people have ever heard any of those details," Whip replied. "Classified."

For a long time, Bravo stood in silence, staring at the controls of the skipper. Eventually he gave a shake of the head and started the repulsor motor back up. That was when April bolted out of the skipper and onto the terrace.

"Wait!" She ran to an overgrown mound and began rolling the ever-present vines off to one side. "This may be what I'm looking for. It is!"

She had revealed a slanted metal grate, with vents connected to a tunnel that led into the heart of the terrace's main body. She tried several times to work the handle's lock, but it would not budge. Finally, she picked up a rock and began hammering at it.

"Hold on," Bravo took the rock from her hand. "If you damage the locking mechanism, we'll never get this open."

"But it already won't open," April argued, "the only way to get it working is to break it. This tunnel probably runs for a mile before it intersects with the one where my people are hiding. *No one* will hear us knocking."

"Lonan," Bravo called Mcguffin over. "You were pretty good with locked doors on Ansa. Want to try your hand with this one?"

"The locks on Ansa were keyed to sound," Lonan replied. "I doubt singing a tune will work, but I'll take a look."

Lonan hummed to himself as he studied the door and its frame for several minutes, confirming that there were no outer hinges that he could break. When he began running his fingers across the locking mechanism, something inside the lock emitted a popping sound. The handle turned on its own and the door snapped ajar.

With an easy pull, Lonan opened the way away.

"How did you do that?" Bravo asked.

"I only touched it," Lonan replied.

April's expression of infatuation had changed to

one of distrust when she looked at Lonan again.

"You're a Terraformer," she asserted.

"No," Lonan protested, and then acquiesced. "Well, yes, by blood only. My name is Mcguffin, with a lower case G. Lonan Mcguffin."

"That explains it," April replied. "My father told a story about how every lock ever built by the Terraformers, everywhere throughout the stars, can be opened by a member the Terraformers' head family, the Mcguffins, with just a touch."

"Genetic locks," Whip confirmed. "I'd heard the rumors, but never believed them."

"Yes," said April. "The legend that the Terraformers built a backdoor key into every settlement that they ever constructed is true. My Daddy was stranded here because we knew the truth about that, and other things even more secret."

Before either Whip or Bravo could ask any further questions, April had plunged into the inky darkness of the tunnel.

"Follow my voice," she called out as Lonan trailed her, followed by Bravo carrying the disabled Daestar with her arms slung over his shoulder like a baby who needed burping, so that one hand was free to feel the way.

Whip stayed at the rear, reaching through the vent slats to try to return the covering vines to their original positions. But he did leave one decent sliver that he was confident would reveal no metal, but still provided the spelunkers with one ray of starlight, dim as it might be.

He was more than a little disorientated when he turned to follow, placing his hands out to either side and taking one tentative step in front of the other until he found the tunnel side. Quickening his step, he hurried to catch up to the sound of soft footfalls in front of him.

"Everyone doesn't need to go all quiet now," he said.

"Yes," Bravo answered, "we do. We don't know what's in here."

They did not have to travel far in the darkness before dim fluorescent bulbs in the ceiling flickered to life. Whip marveled at the ancient technology that he had read about but never before seen. Still, their use was different than shown in the history books. Instead of hanging openly from the ceiling, the bulbs were placed in a chamber behind a thick, quartz-like barrier that both shielded the bulbs and radiated their light.

"Terraformers never put the switches near the door," April explained, "as a way of keeping intruders out."

Bravo shifted Daestar to where he cradled her with both arms, leaning her head against his shoulder.

"You think she saw Erlik die?" he asked Whip.

"Pretty sure."

"Poor girl," Bravo replied. "I know what it's like, watching someone you love die before your eyes."

Daestar's eyes blinked several times.

"You still in there?" Bravo asked. "Good."

They reached a junction where the lights were out.

"That's odd," said April. "This far in, the lights are always motion activated."

Then the lights behind them also went out.

"Nobody move," Bravo warned.

"Good advice," boomed a voice through the darkness.

When the lights returned abruptly, Whip discovered a handmade knife held to his throat. He stood in the center of a tunnel junction inhabited by dozens of malnourished people who looked on with glowering eyes. Whip had silently despaired over the suffering he had seen on Earth, but what he saw now took the definition of *destitute* to another level. Families huddled together by the tunnel's sides where bare cots were arranged in tents too small to cover them completely. Their clothes were the rags of multiple shirts that had been combined repeatedly. No one wore shoes.

Six of the men also moved in to threaten Bravo and Lonan.

Only April stood free.

"Daddy!" she cried out and ran to hug the man threatening Whip. "I've missed you!"

"What are you doing here?" he snarled, pushing the edge of his blade even closer. "Who are these people? Pirates?"

"No, Daddy," April scoffed. "Look at them."

"I am," her father replied, "and this one looks like the head of the Artomiques."

"I was supposed to be," said Whip. "But I'm not. Never was."

"What is that supposed to mean?"

Whip had no response. He noticed how all the men seemed to be about the same age as Bravo, and thought for a minute how he had never been around so many old people, until he realized that his body was even older than theirs.

"You!" Bravo interjected as he leaned Daestar against the wall, drawing no objection from the man aiming a sharpened pipe at him. "Move closer to the light—where I can see your face."

"Move closer to the light, yourself," April's father haughtily asserted.

Bravo stepped forward, keeping his hands held high and far away from the injector knife at his hip.

"You're Rock Candy," he said, "aren't you? Until I saw you just now, I thought her name of April Candy was a joke."

"How do you know me?" Rock backed the blade a few inches away from Whip's throat. "I don't recognize you."

"You wouldn't," Bravo replied. "When I was involved in negotiations with the Terraformers, I did my research. You're a legend in their history. It's been said that there was no engineering challenge that you couldn't master. It was also said you died twenty years ago."

Much to Whip's relief, Rock stepped away and sheathed his blade. He waved his arm about in a lateral circle.

"You're looking at my last project," said Rock. "A world with an engine built by a long lost people. No one thought it could be made to work again. But I found a way. This whole place was built with technology that could have advanced Earth by millennia. Yet no one knows a thing about it other than me."

"So what happened?" Bravo asked. "You're right about how no one has ever heard of this place. Corsairiana is one of the biggest secrets of the stars. Why did you disappear? It was right about the time

that his father," Bravo nodded toward Lonan, "split with the Terraformers."

"Are you a Darklaw?" Rock demanded with a tightened grip on his blade. "It was Raider Darklaw, on his very first project as a supervisor, who stranded us here after construction was completed. "

"No," Bravo replied. "My name is Bully Bravo, and..."

"He used to be the President of the United States on Earth," April excitedly interrupted him. She gave Bravo a sly smile and a wink.

"All the Darklaws are dead," Bravo ignored April and finished his sentence.

She made a pouty face in reaction to his lack of response.

"Really?" Rock displayed his first smile. "How? Did the pirates turn on him? Or did his father finally learn he was betraying the Terraformers to the pirates, and kill Raider himself?"

"Actually," said Bravo, "he was eaten by an extra-dimensional entity that Raider loosed on our universe with wormhole technology."

Rock had no reply. His jaw went slack and his eyes blinked rapidly.

"Why were you stranded here?" Whip asked.

"That Red Bitch who calls herself a Queen was worried that we might reveal this world's secrets. How can you reveal a world that has the ability to relocate itself?"

"Apparently," said Bravo, "they've been having trouble with that part. They stole a massive power coupling to get that world engine running again."

Rock's face went pale.

"They won't know how to install it!" He looked around in a panic. "They'll be after us again... after me! We've got to hide! Go even deeper into the engine's vents!"

Bravo caught his arm as women and children began hurriedly bundling their belongings.

"Instead of running," he suggested, "why not take the fight to them?"

"How can they do that?" Whip asked.

Bravo looked directly at Lonan, and then back to Whip.

"They've now got two things that they've never

had before. They've got Lonan, who can open the doors into the Citadel, and they've got your face, Whip. Judging by April's reactions, the pirates still believe you're Achilles Hister."

"I'm still not convinced he isn't," Rock grumbled.

"The Citadel has no access except at the very top," said Whip.

"Oh, but it does," said Rock. "The foundation is tied into the same vent network that we're standing in. The planetary engine generates a lot of heat, which the Citadel was built to recycle and store as energy."

"You can walk into the Citadel's command center and order them to disarm their planetary defense systems," Bravo said to Whip.

"What good will that do?" asked Rock.

"Because, while you, Whip, were unpacking a Splendora bot ..."

The name Splendora was murmured by every man present.

"That model has been a top seller for some time," Whip felt compelled to explain their reaction.

"And while you, Lonan," Bravo continued, "were helping Roy and Pam prepare to hijack that heavy-duty hauler and the power coupling, I did a little hijacking of my own. I sent a low-frequency MagLink signal with the coordinates of this world to the military gathered around Nebula 71. By my calculations, they should arrive here around dawn."

Rock blinked several times, looked around to April and his men, then back to Bravo.

"If what you say is true, then all we need to do is lay low until the fighting is over."

"There's no guarantee that Earth's military will win this fight. There's an Artomique Dreadnaught of a new design in orbit. No one knows what it's capable of. You could still end up spending the rest of your lives hiding down here in these vents—and being burnt to a crisp if they ever get the planetary engine operating again."

"Oh... we can hear the engine when it starts up. Gives us plenty of time to clear out. We're usually not as settled in as we are now," Rock gestured at the makeshift tents and sleeping mattresses, "because it's been a while."

"My point is—your odds of getting off this world become a whole lot better if you'd lend a hand. Or, better yet, you could make this world your own. After all, you're the one who built it. Wasn't the issue of never getting to claim your work for your own part of the whole schism that caused Lonan's father to break off from the rest of you?"

"What about her?" Whip nodded at Daestar, slumped against the wall, but her eyes still alert as she watched everything going on around her. "You need to get her off this world, find her some help."

"There's no one here that could help her," April confirmed. "She's going to die a slow and wasting death, unless you know of anyone who can undo the Red Queen's handiwork?"

"Yeah," Bravo confirmed. "I know a guy. But I'd need a really good starship to reach him."

"We can help," said Lonan. "Candy, do these tunnels run all the way to the upper terraces?"

"Yes. I grew up in these tunnels. I know them better than anyone. But that way has a lot of locks..." She paused and looked at Lonan. "...which isn't be a problem for you, is it?"

"Then we have a plan," Whip asserted. "Lonan gets me and Rock inside the Citadel, and then he gets you to the Gravedigger. I'll make sure that Corsairiana falls with as little resistance as possible."

Rock shook his head.

"A lot of things can go wrong with that plan."

"But a lot can go right," April tugged on her father's arm. "You don't really want to keep living down here in the darkness, do you? Mommy's last words were about wanting to feel sunlight on her face again."

Rock gave a forlorn look around at his people.

"There used to be a hundred of us," he said.

Whip thought he heard someone whisper, and turned to realize that Daestar was desperately trying to speak. Bravo had heard it, too, and was already leaning low, putting his ear next to her mouth. She repeated herself several times.

"Red Queen," he announced the warning after wiping a bit of drool from the corner of Daestar's mouth.

"Not a problem," Whip asserted. "I don't know

how I did it, but earlier my mind put up some kind of mental barrier that blocked her out. That's how I escaped the Citadel. Now that I know what I'm doing, she'll be no problem."

"Just don't get overconfident." Bravo seemed to notice how devastated Whip was when April ran to Lonan.

"I don't want you to go," she urged Lonan.

"After we get Daestar to where someone can help her, I'll come back," Lonan promised.

"I thought she liked me," Whip confided to Bravo in a low voice. "I thought we'd made a connection."

"Believe me," Bravo whispered back, "a girl like that changes her affections like the wind changes directions. If you decide to stay, remember that after we're gone and the wind shifts again."

Chapter Thirteen:
Return of an Old Friend

"You know," Bully Bravo said, "for our plan to work, the Red Queen has to be put down."

Whip's footfalls echoed along the upward slant of the tunnel as he labored to keep up with April, who was led the way. A Daestar-laden Bravo stayed on his shoulder, seemingly unfazed by her weight or the pace of the climb.

"After what she did to me," Whip glanced at the brown spots on the back of his hand, and then at the injector blade hanging at Bravo's hip, "you'd think I would be the first to tie a loop in the hangman's noose. But there's got to be an alternative."

"I wish there was," Bravo replied.

"Found it!" April declared as she stopped and pointed to a locked gate on one side of a junction. "That way leads back to the terraces where you killed Takeshak."

"You killed Takeshak?" Rock could be heard from the back of the half dozen men he had brought, all of them carrying steel pipes with sharpened points and makeshift knives. "I'm beginning to like these guys."

Before Lonan could touch the lock, Rock pushed his way to the forefront.

"I've got to see this," he demanded. "I won't

believe it unless I do."

Lonan did not even look where he reached, staring at Rock when the locking mechanism released at the touch his hand.

"It's true," Rock was astonished. "Kid, there is nowhere—anywhere—that you can't go."

Bravo gently placed Daestar down in a sitting position. She seemed to be slowly regaining some of her motor function and dropped her hands to the tunnel floor to support herself in a sitting position.

"This tunnel," said Bravo, "this is mostly Wild Stars design..."

"Wild Stars?" Rock scoffed. "You believe those old stories?"

"Oh, those stories are real," said Whip.

"In the years since you've been gone," said Lonan, "the universe has changed. And I don't think the Red Queen likes it."

"Why did you put in so many locked gates?" Bravo asked. "I can understand why you put in the antique lighting, but why add all the gates?"

"It's what the Red Queen wanted," Rock replied. "She has... had... the only key. And the metal we used on the gates is hell to cut. Takes tools we don't have."

"Are there many gates between here and the terrace with the landing pad?"

"No one knows," said April. "Never been down that way, but probably. Probably a lot."

"Then that makes our plan simple," said Bravo. "We'll leave Daestar here. Lonan, after you get us into the Citadel, you beat feet back here and get Daestar and yourself to the Gravedigger. I'll find my own way off world once we've dealt with the Red Queen."

Daestar shook her head as best she could, and once again began murmuring the name, "Red Queen."

"That's pretty amazing," said April. "I've never seen anyone be able to speak, let alone regain any movement, after the Red Queen got done with them."

"I'm not going to forget about you," Bravo knelt down to Daestar and gripped her shoulders for reassurance. "But the Gravedigger won't get away unless the Red Queen is dealt with. Rock, leave a lantern here with her."

"Why?" he asked.

"These lights are motion-activated, and as you can see, Daestar isn't real active right now. I don't want her waiting here alone in the dark."

"Nothing can get her," April admonished. "We're the only things that have ever come into these tunnels."

Whip recoiled at the stern expression that etched across Bravo's face when he glared at April and Rock.

Without another word, a bright lantern was activated and placed at Daestar's feet.

As they walked away, they could hear her continue to call the Red Queen.

"Think that's a warning?" Whip asked.

"Probably," Bravo replied.

There was little conversation as they continued their climb up the tunnels, their combined footfalls and labored breath multiplying as the acoustics echoed down the tunnel.

"There!" April pointed haughtily at a certain gate when all were paused at the next junction.

"You've got a good sense of direction," Bravo complimented her.

Whip saw that, after the incident with the lantern, April now seemed irritated with anything that Bravo said. Apparently, Bravo picked up on it too and did not try to speak to her again.

There was no doubt when they reached the next locked door. The red wall before them could only belong to the foundation of the Citadel.

Lonan hesitated at the lock on the vented gate.

"We're ready," Rock hissed as he and his men pushed close to Lonan's back, their weapons held ready.

When they passed through the gates, they had to activate their lanterns. Their shadows stretched long and danced eerily across the walls of what looked like a catacomb. Only upon closer inspection did Whip realize that the foundation was honeycombed with vents to transfer heat upwards into the Citadel.

April moved unerringly forward and quickly found another gate that led to a circular metal stairwell. It led them to a long hallway with another gate at the far end. Along the walls leading that way were numerous other gates, but these did not guard tunnels.

"These are prisons," Bravo said the words like a curse.

"Bully?" a faint voice echoed out of the darkness of the nearest cell. "Is that really you?"

Lonan moved to unlock the gate and Bravo pushed past, disappearing into the cell's inky darkness. When he emerged, he was once again carrying a nearly helpless woman, but this time she had dark hair and Japanese features. Her body was emaciated from starvation.

"Topeka Tanaka," asked Bravo, "how did you get here?"

"The Red Queen didn't want someone familiar with her sister running around loose," she replied in a faint voice.

"What did she do to you?"

"When the Red Queen is planning on executing a prisoner," she replied, her eyes gazed adoringly up at his, "they stop feeding you. That's how you know when your time is up."

Bravo nodded for Rock's men to check the other cells. They were all unlocked with no one inside.

"Who the hello is she?" Rock asked Whip.

"That's Topeka Tanaka," Lonan answered. "I met her and Bully when they were shipwrecked on Ansa. Her brother, Tijuana Tanaka..."

"He was an outstanding baseball pitcher," Whip interjected.

"Tijuana was the Red Queen's boyfriend," Lonan finished.

"One of them," Whip added.

"One of her boyfriends?" Rock confirmed.

"No," Whip replied. "One of the Red Queens."

"You mean there's more than one of them?"

"Not anymore," said Whip. "One of the sisters was eaten by a red grief, on Akara's World."

"I thought that was just a rumor?" asked Lonan.

"Not according to an actor named Fuzzy..."

Before Whip could say another word, the metallic sound of the lock turning on the gate at the far end of the tunnel impelled Lonan, Rock, and all the

Terraformers to hide in the darkness of the cells.

"Looks like the Red Queen is coming to claim her," Rock whispered as he disappeared into Topeka's cell.

Whip stood his ground in front of where an angry Bravo still knelt, not even attempting to move as he cradled Topeka in his arms.

When several pirates entered the hall, they were surprised to see intruders and reached for their weapons.

"Everyone," Whip raised a hand in a stop gesture, "weapons down! Come here. There is something you need to explain to me."

Whip pointed at the open door of Topeka's cell. The confused pirates obviously recognized him but still kept their weapons ready, although lowered, seeing no threat from Bully or Topeka. With Whip mostly blocking their view, all they saw was the injector knife at Bravo's side and they thought him a fellow pirate. Still, they kept an eye on him when they neared and peered inside Topeka's cell. By the time they realized it was a trap—it was too late.

The fury of the attack by Rock and others, going instantly for the pirate's throats with their pointed pipes and blades, shocked Whip with its violence and complete lack of mercy. It revealed to him the intensity of the Terraformers' rage and desperation after having lived so many years in hiding.

"Their clothes," Whip took a ringed set of keys off the pirate who had opened the door. "Get them on. Pass pieces around to everyone. Don't worry about the blood."

"You know," Lonan said to Bravo as he looked at Topeka with great concern, "we've got to get her out of here."

Bravo hesitated.

"We've got a job to do," he replied.

"Yes," Whip continued to assert himself. "We've got our job, and you've got yours. Two women are in desperate need and require your help, Mister President. Lonan can't carry them both. What are you still doing here? We don't need you. I've got this."

With keys in hand, and without waiting for a reply or reaction, Whip led the band of Terraformers, now dressed as pirates, to the stairwell at the tunnel's far end. But before he started his next ascent, Whip paused to look behind him.

Lonan, Bravo, and Topeka were nowhere to be seen.

"Aww," April pouted when she noticed.

Chapter Fourteen:
The Checkmate Weapon Unleashed

When the Red Queen had attacked, Daestar's instinctive defenses saved her mind from total destruction, but not by much.

Daestar was thrown into an empty cell of her own mind. Her eyes were still an open window to the world, but her mind was barely able to comprehend what she saw.

She felt as though she was caught in a dream, futilely trying to wake herself, but unable to control any of her motor functions. Desperately, she endeavored to move a finger or twitch a muscle in her legs.

The battle back into consciousness was like a long climb out of a ravine. She slowly began to understand a smattering of what was happening around her when she heard Whip foolishly state that he felt he could defend himself from a psychic attack by the Red Queen.

Try as she might, no one heard her calling out a warning. They seemed to notice that she was trying to communicate, but it was like speaking in a dream where no words can be heard. Finally, she managed to shape the words, "Red Queen," but it was a faint whisper that those around her disregarded.

She did feel slightly reassured when Bravo picked her up and carried her, but then he took her even deeper into the bowels of Corsairiana and abandoned her.

A wave of panic hit when the tunnel lights flickered and went out, but the blackness was not complete, as a lantern at her feet shone like a beacon.

Never had she felt so alone. Never before had she been in an environment of complete silence. She had always had to shield herself from the cacophony of thoughts and words of those surrounding her. But even when Bravo had carried her, he was like a blank slate. No one she had ever met was capable of forming such a complete stone wall.

Now she was left empty and alone like never before.

Her motor function was slowly coming back, and she no longer felt asleep. It was getting her body to respond that became the next problem.

For a long time, Daestar sat there, working on getting one muscle after another to twitch, and then getting her arms and legs to move. Finally, she was able to lurch clumsily, with her back against the tunnel, and force herself to her feet.

Suddenly the tunnel lights returned.

She tried several times unsuccessfully to pick up the lantern. Eventually, she was able to keep her grip and look around with a bare amount of cognitive ability. Only then did she wonder why she had bothered with the lantern when there was now light.

Daestar recognized that she was in the vent tunnels of a planetary engine's exhaust network and began to panic. For a moment she thought that she was somehow back in the heart of the Devil's Delight, but then remembered how that rogue planet had been detonated by the Ancient Warrior when he destroyed a Brothan invasion armada.

An open gate loomed before her. She had no idea about which direction Bravo had gone, but she knew that he was headed into a danger that he and Whip were incapable of defending themselves against, and they were going to need her help.

Determining that the gate must be open for a reason, and that she had been left behind for her own protection, Daestar stumbled across the tunnel and grasped the grating in the door before she fell.

But no lights activated within the tunnel when she entered, and she was glad that she had never released the lantern.

With one foot slowly placed in front the other, she staggered and bounced off the tunnel walls, desperate to stop Bravo from walking into his doom.

After what seemed like a long journey, though she knew her distorted senses must have exaggerated it in her perception, Daestar came to another gate, this one closed.

Pulling on the grating, Daestar could not get the door open. She held the light near the lock, and then dropped it in fear and shock.

Right next to the lock, a hand reached in her direction through the grating. Only after the initial shock had passed did she realize that the hand was lifeless and nearly skeletal, with the flesh dried and shriveled around the bone. Someone had been locked on the other side and abandoned. That they had died there told Daestar that there was yet another locked gate further down the tunnel.

She had gone the wrong way.

Daestar slowly picked the lantern back up and began to turn when she heard the sound of heavy footsteps and even heavier breathing.

With her head bowed because she could not fully raise it, Daestar leaned against the gate's grating and awaited her fate.

A voice called out before the approaching man entered the field of light created by the lantern.

"Daestar!" Lonan hurried into view, rushing to support her before she fell. "I don't know what's wrong with the lights, but it worked out. I saw the glow from your lantern."

His words barely registered with her. All she was cognizant of was that she was no longer all alone but could sense none of Lonan's thoughts. Still, she was thankful for his presence.

Then Lonan spotted the emaciated hand and the mummified body on the other side of the gate.

"Damn," he cursed. "Starving someone to death isn't enough for the Red Queen. Imprisoning them in a tomb of darkness while they starve goes beyond cruel! Bravo was right about how she needs to be dealt with."

Daestar had no idea what Lonan was referencing, but she felt as though it was something she should know. It was an uncomfortable feeling.

"Which way?" Bravo's voice barreled down the tunnel.

Lonan called him down, looking fairly surprised when Bravo appeared out of the darkness, carrying what looked like a child in his arms.

"I thought you would've seen the same glow that I did," he said.

"Kid," said Bravo, "you've got the eyesight of

someone who's lived most of his life in the wild, and the legs, too. You went off and left me like I was standing still."

"I wasn't carrying someone," Lonan replied.

"Well, you're going to be helping carry someone now. Get it back in gear and get that gate unlocked. Don't worry about that dead man. Daestar, I'm glad to see you back in the land of the living."

Daestar waved a hand, still lacking her vocal skills.

Once Lonan touched the lock, Bravo kicked the gate open and the body to one side without a second glance, calling for Lonan to bring Daestar and her lantern.

They passed through several more gates, and by more bodies, before they encountered one with a wall of vines on the other side. Lonan tugged on several of them, but without access to the roots, he found them impossible to remove.

"It's impenetrable. These aren't loose like the ones on that other gate. They seem older and thicker. There's no flexibility at all."

"Out of my way."

Bravo set his passenger on the floor and leaned her against Daestar's legs. For the first time, Daestar had a good look at her, but still did not recognize her face. It became obvious that this was a woman, not a child, though there were evident signs of starvation. She was clearly another victim of the Red Queen.

Bravo pulled the injector knife.

The combination of the huge blade's sharp edge and the freezing component being injected into the cuts made their final exit short work.

Soon, they stood beneath the many moons of Corsairiana, with the Gravedigger only a short distance away.

"Is everyone ready?" Bravo asked after double-tapping the transponder in his ear.

"Still here," said Pam Kerk.

"Me, too," said Roy Kerk. "I've got the heavy hauler attached to the power coupling. We're itching to go."

"No one ever came knocking," Pam added.

"Yeah," said Bravo, "they wouldn't have. Whip killed their leader."

"What?" Pam sounded astonished.

"A pirate named Slane Takeshak," Lonan explained. "Without a leader, I'm sure the pirates have spent the whole night entertaining themselves with the Splendora."

"Well," said Pam, "at least you didn't call that thing by my name! You folks better hurry. That Lantern Star is getting ready to light up the sky."

"We're at the Gravedigger now," said Bravo. "Open up. Roy, do you want me or Lonan to help you?"

"I've got this," said Roy as the heavy hauler's engines lit up and the ship began to slowly rise, being careful with its attitude so as not to tangle the lifting cables.

Daestar paused at the Gravedigger's hatch when Bravo stopped to watch the hauler lift off. The starved woman tried to keep a grip on Bravo when Lonan took her from his arms and carried her inside.

"Watch your tilt," Bravo warned as Roy made quick adjustments, and soon, the cables were taut, and the power coupling stood in a vertical position. "You're good to go."

As soon as the hatch shut behind them, the Gravedigger lifted into the air. Bravo caught Daestar before the jolt threw her to the floor.

Daestar was led to the cockpit and placed into a seat next to the strange woman.

"Meet Topeka Tanaka," said Bravo. "Topeka, this is Daestar. You're both some of my best friends."

Topeka's head lolling about as the ship tilted to a steep ascent. Bravo joined Pam at the controls, while Lonan hurried to find food and water for Topeka.

The Gravedigger moved in front of Roy's heavy hauler, allowing it to wind-draft behind them.

"Oh, oh."

Pam's reaction pulled Daestar's eyes in the same direction as hers.

The Artomique dreadnought that had been sitting stationary in orbit was now moving to intercept, her belly painted by waves of golden light as the Lantern Star crested on the horizon.

"That's not the worst of it." Bravo brought up a

rear-view image on the monitor. Below them, pirate ships were scrambling all across the landing field they had just left. "They'll get to us before we ever make orbit. Either Whip hasn't made it to the top of the Citadel yet, or he's dead. I was worried that there was something off about that April girl."

Daestar's heart began to pound. The Red Queen had taken so much from her. Now her victory would be complete.

"We can't let this happen!" she managed a burst of speech.

"Yipper, but not a lot we can do about it," said Bravo. "Lonan, get on that cannon! At least we can go down fighting!"

Arriving just outside the doorway of the bridge, Lonan darted in, dumped the food and drink he carried into Topeka's lap, and ran back out.

Daestar helped Topeka work the canister of water open and then had to keep her from gulping the contents down whole.

"Take it easy," Bravo cautioned.

The ship rocked violently when percussion blasts bracketed them and pieces of shrapnel ricocheted loudly off the viewports.

"They're trying to force us down," Bravo warned. "Don't do it. Better to die up here than down there at the mercy of the Red Queen. I've seen enough of what a pirate Queen does to her prisoners."

Several pirate ships shot past them, with the Gravedigger being limited by the speed of the heavy hauler and its weighty load creeping slowly up behind them.

"Don't wait for me," Roy's voice rang in their ears.

Bravo pulled out his earplug and opened up a communications link on the control console.

"We're not leaving you," he asserted.

"That's right," Pam echoed.

She gave Bravo a look of fright and uncertainty.

Then one of the ships blocking their way exploded into flames and began to fall as a smoking wreck.

"Keep it up, Lonan!" Bravo urged.

"It wasn't me," Lonan replied. "I'm just now strapping into the turret."

Another ship exploded behind them, followed by another and then another. No two ships exploded at the same time, further confusing the pirates, who turned their ships and fled.

"They think we've got a Checkmate Weapon!" Roy called out.

A delayed cascade effect seemed to shimmer across the sky as the pirate ships fell one after another in flames. One made it back to the ground, only to detonate before the crew could disembark.

"The Splendora," Bravo conjectured. "Are you seeing this, Roy? That could have been you!"

"Did Whip program her to be a killer?" Pam asked.

"I doubt it," Bravo replied. "She was probably already programmed that way. But... he is an Artomique."

Chapter Fifteen:
Assault on the Red Citadel

"Artomique in the room!" Rock announced as he followed Whip into the command center.

Whip had given the double doors a push that was a touch too sensitive and they bounced back on him, causing the pirates guarding either side to give him a look of surprise, but they did nothing to intervene. The rest of Rock's men remained outside, ready to provide backup.

"Where's that fire coming from?" A frantic controller ignored them as he paced back and forth behind several seated men, pointing at the multiple ships taking turns exploding in the sky. "They've got some sort of secret weapon. Look, they're even killing them as they run away. That ship is crewed by monsters! Get everyone up in the air from all the landing fields!"

"Cancel that order!" Whip commanded in an authoritative voice.

The controller stopped and stared as every member of the command crew watched and waited for the controller's instructions.

Then there came the sound of a heavy object falling in the hallway just outside the doorway. That sound was followed by a second object striking the floor.

The doors were flung open in a dramatic fashion

as the Red Queen strutted through, waving a bloodied knife to indicate for the guards to seize Whip and Rock. In the hallway behind her, two men lay lifeless on the floor, blood oozing from their necks.

"Don't worry," the Red Queen indicated the rest of the men, who stood counting their fingers in a dazed stupor. "I've saved the rest to use as incentive, now that I have you back, Rock. Hello again, Whip."

April caught one of the doors before it closed and entered, a broad smile etched across her face.

"You did well, child," said the Red Queen.

"He ordered me to ground all our ships," the controller explained when the Red Queen looked at the empty monitor screen. "That escaping ship knocked everyone else out of the sky. They've got some sort of Checkmate Weapon like we've never seen before!"

"Then leave it be," said the Red Queen as she tapped a control console and threw an orbital shot onto the room's center hologram, focusing on the Artomique dreadnought. "It's time for our friends to show us what they can do."

As the dreadnought moved into position to meet the Gravedigger head-on, a smaller ship launched from her midsection and headed down, passing the rising ships on a parallel trajectory.

Every time the Gravedigger shifted direction, the dreadnought moved to match it. It appeared to be aiming to ram the Gravedigger head-on when they once again changed course. This time, the heavy hauler did not match the change and made a break for open space.

The dreadnought maintained its course to intercept the Gravedigger.

"The 'scary President' is on that ship," said April.

"Good," the Red Queen replied.

"And a Mcguffin, he can unlock any door anywhere with just a touch."

"Even better. Someone like that is too dangerous to live."

Whip's arms were held firmly, so he tried to exert his newfound mental skills, and instantly a wall of mental crystal surrounded him.

The Red Queen noticed his psychic barrier. She looked at him, smiled, and then waved the bloody knife so that a spatter of blood flew in his direction. The blood crashed through his psychic shield, shattering it like glass before striking him in the face.

"Fool," he heard in his mind, "I don't need to control you. There's nothing you can do."

"Ha!" Whip laughed as he watched the Gravedigger bounce away from the myriad weapons and grasping appendages deploying from the Godspeed's prow. The Gravedigger escaped in a shower of sparks as the dreadnought was deflected by a blast from an Earth military ship that popped suddenly into orbit. "Looks like I did enough."

Waves of Earth's military craft followed in behind the first, filling the sky above Corsairiana.

"Tell everyone to stand down," the Red Queen ordered. "No one fires a shot. Give my guests in the Godspeed's shuttle time to reach me."

The control room monitors and speakers began to fill with the image of one man.

"This is Admiral Bryce," his voice echoed from all the different displays. "I'm ordering every ship in orbit to land immediately and submit to our search and seizure."

"No response," ordered the Red Queen.

Bryce repeated his command several times. By the time he was issuing his final warning, the room's double doors had opened once again, and Whip saw himself enter the room—or rather he saw his former body under the control of his father.

"Hello, Son," said Achilles.

The Red Queen strode forward, embracing Achilles with a passionate kiss.

"That's so much better," she said with a smile. "You and I are going to have so much fun!"

"I brought a couple of presents for you," said Achilles. "Send them in!"

A pair of Artomique crewmen held open the doors, revealing the stupefied Terraformers still staggering about the hall. A tall, young, blond-haired man and woman who looked to be twins, dressed in makeshift armor and clothes that were cobbled together from dozens of different cultures walked past them.

"Allow me to introduce Mackstar and Akarastar,"

said Achilles. "They were riding in a commandeered miner's tug, and a very slow one, at that, and wouldn't have reached the Orbital Relay Station for several weeks if we hadn't offered our assistance. They've come as representatives of Akara's World—I mean Miri—so we brought them here." He noted their look of irritation. "Miri wants to join our rebellion against Earth."

"It looks like we've joined the losing side," said Mackstar, listening to monitors where Bryce had begun a final countdown for Corsairiana's surrender.

"Nonsense," said the Red Queen. "Looks can be deceiving." She then walked over to Akarastar and caressed her cheek with one hand. "I really need to introduce you to my mother."

"Don't trust her!" Whip shouted. "She wants your bodies! She'll steal them," he pointed to Achilles, "just like Dad took mine!"

"Poor boy," said April. "He's a delusional Earth spy sent to disable our defenses for their invasion. He'll say anything."

She sneered when she saw Whip's look of disappointment.

"Looks like the wind just shifted again."

His words seemed to confuse April.

The Red Queen laughed softly and took a ballistic handgun from one of her guards.

"One thing that my sister and I both had in common," she placed the tip of the gun barrel between Whip's unflinching eyes, "is that we both always liked doing the dirty work ourselves. Part of the reason why I'm called the Red Queen is because I enjoy being covered with other people's blood."

He saw her hand tense as the gun's barrel rotated, but did not see it fire. Hearing the explosion was his last conscious sensation.

Chapter Sixteen:
Escape From Corsairiana

Daestar felt like a helpless spectator as she watched the Surface To Space shuttle launch from the Artomique dreadnought, Godspeed, and take a reverse parallel course to that of the Gravedigger, passing right next to them.

"Any idea who's on board that thing?" Bully Bravo looked at her.

Daestar shook her head.

"I'm lucky to be getting my movement and speech back," she replied in a weak voice that steadily grew stronger. "But my mind is deaf. The world around me has gone silent. Everything is so… quiet."

Pam repeatedly changed course, always advising Roy in advance.

"Stop that," said Bravo as the Godspeed loomed in front of them, always matching the Gravedigger's every movement. "Send him the opposite way next time."

The ploy worked, with Roy's heavy hauler headed on an unimpeded course out of orbit and into deep space. The Godspeed continued to maintain a collision course with the Gravedigger.

"They're concentrating on us," said Bravo. "With that heavy load, that hauler is so slow—they're planning on running Roy down later."

"What are they doing?" Pam asked when the Godspeed seemed to shiver. Then she screamed, "Oh, my God!"

The Godspeed's prow began to separate into four sections, opening up to reveal an array of cutting lasers and grinders large enough to disassemble any spaceship. That array began to extend outward like a pharyngeal jaw.

"They've made the biggest salvage ship ever!" Pam shouted.

"No," said Bravo. "They've tried to recreate Zarawti, the space shark that eats spaceships. Pam! Cut loose with that cannon!"

Plasma bolts began disappearing into the maw of the Godspeed, causing little or no damage. This was a machine designed to be impervious as it dealt out destruction to explosive components.

Pam repeatedly tried to change course and juke away from the massive vessel, but the Godspeed's flexible body design made it uncannily agile. The maw was about to close on the Gravedigger when a powerful energy blast struck the Godspeed's side. The blast knocked her off course, but not quite enough to be clear of the Gravedigger.

Grinders gouged and sparked all along the salvage ship's side but did not penetrate the hull, as the action effectively knocked the Gravedigger free and clear.

Pam hastily set a course to follow Roy into deep space as Earth military ships appeared from every direction, moving into orbit around Corsairiana and providing a metal wall of protection that enabled the Gravedigger to escape.

"Where the hello did those come from?" Pam asked.

"I sent them a signal," said Bravo, "while you and Roy were helping Whip unpack the Splendora."

"You sneaky little bastard," Pam retorted. "I love it!"

Bravo brought up a view of the showdown between the Earth's military and the pirate fleet on the main monitor.

"Looks like the pirates know they're beat," he said. "They're not resisting at all. Looks like Earth sent every ship in the region."

A long standoff then ensued.

"Should we wait and watch the show?" Pam asked.

"Keep Roy's hauler moving as fast as it can go," Bravo replied. "Something about this worries me. Tell him to head in the direction of Nebula 71."

"What?" Pam called out.

"Don't go into it," Bravo explained. "But let's head in that direction. We might need the cover if something goes wrong."

"What could go wrong?" Pam asked with a sarcastic tone.

"Never underestimate the Red Queen," Daestar finally found the strength to speak again, as she endeavored to help the equally weak Topeka take a tiny bite of food.

As the Gravedigger and heavy hauler passed the Lantern Star, they could finally see through the optical illusion; the two stars were locked in a death spiral but not yet merged. They rotated so close to each other that their spin created the appearance of a lantern shape.

"Here comes the cavalry," Pam called out.

The Gravedigger's main monitor had switched to a long-range view when waves of massive Artomique ships suddenly began dropping from hyper-light speeds as they slammed into Corsairiana's orbit directly behind the Earth fleet.

"Where did they come from?" Bravo asked no one in particular, his voice growing tense.

"You don't sound happy to see them?"

"Didn't you notice what the Godspeed just tried to do to us?" Bravo nodded to another monitor that showed a service droid crawling along the Gravedigger's exterior, meticulously pumping sealant to reinforce the rows of grooves recently etched across the hull.

"That looks like a bite from a shark," Topeka whispered to Daestar.

"You okay?" Bravo turned his attention to Topeka. "We've been running since I found you. I haven't had time to ask. How's Fuzzy? Did they get him, too?"

"Fuzzy?" Topeka asked in reply. "What would the Red Queen want with Fuzzy? Unless... you think she wants to kill anyone who saw what she did to my brother?"

"He was just checking," Daestar smiled as she intervened for Bravo, not needing her telepathic skills to recognize that Topeka had never realized Fuzzy's fondness for her—just as Bravo had never seemed to notice the same thing from Topeka.

"I've got bad news," said Pam. "Those dreadnoughts just sent a text-only message to Earth's fleet. They say that the Godspeed has gone rogue and warn that Corsairiana has some sort of secret weapon. They got all their defenses set forward and recommend everyone else do so."

"No!" Bravo growled as he lunged for the MagLink panel. "Look at the angle the dreadnoughts took for their entry! They've got Earth's fleet locked in a kill zone."

It was already too late.

A glow surrounded Corsairiana like a halo when the Artomique dreadnoughts all opened fire at once on the Armada of Earth ships. It was a bloody massacre, through which the Godspeed and gathered pirate ships sailed untouched as they rose to join the dreadnought fleet.

The onslaught continued in a blaze of brilliant explosions, long after the last Earth ship had been disabled, and continued until there was nothing left intact that could harbor life.

When the barrage finally ended, a cloud of debris hung in orbit that slowly began to spread as smaller pieces pulled away from large wreckage whose orbits were already beginning to decay.

"They've just cut that world off from space, because it's going to be hell piloting a ship through that," Pam quipped to break the silence of the shock. "Or, maybe not."

Several dreadnoughts dropped into orbit in front of the leading edge of the metal cloud, cracked open their prows and began cruising through the twisted wreckage and clearing the clouds away with grinders that broke the components down for recycling.

Pam gasped when several flailing figures wearing spacesuits were gobbled into an iron maw.

A single dreadnought broke away from the hovering fleet and turned in the direction of the Gravedigger.

"Get us into that Nebula," Bravo shouted. "Now!"

"Wasn't it quarantined for a good reason?" Roy called out.

"Sometimes you've got to pick your poison," said Daestar.

"Yipper," Bravo agreed.

Chapter Seventeen:
The Horror in the Nebula

Side by side, the Gravedigger and heavy hauler pierced the outer cloud layers of Nebula 71. Moving with astonishing speed, the dreadnought was already on top of them and braking before entering the nebula behind them.

"Veer off, Roy," Bravo called out. "Run silent, and we'll meet you at your granddaddy's lode in four lengths the time it takes a Splendora to trigger a lover."

"God willing." Pam crossed a finger over her heart and steered in the opposite direction.

Daestar could appreciate how Bravo's simple code might be effective against any eavesdropping equipment. Even without her telepathic skills, she felt amazed at how much she could still understand about the subterfuge of those around her.

"How is the Red Queen still alive?" Topeka asked after Daestar encouraged her to wait a while before eating or drinking any more.

"There were two of them," Daestar explained. "Twins, although I think one is a stronger telepath. She has certainly practiced her skills a lot more."

"Everyone quiet down," said Bravo. "Shut off everything other than air and heat. We're going to float."

"What about me?" Lonan called out.

"Stay in the gun turret," said Bravo. "We need to be ready for anything. I'll spell you in a while."

The flight deck went silent and dark as most of the lights went out. Pam buckled herself into the pilot's seat while Bravo secured the belts on Daestar's and Topeka's seats.

"You don't like to sit, do you?" Topeka squeaked when Bravo rushed off the flight deck.

What followed seemed like an eternity of floating through the shifting colors of the nebula. Eventually, Daestar fell asleep, only to be awakened when Bravo returned to ask Pam to fire the thrusters just enough to level the Gravedigger out and avoid tumbling.

Suddenly, a shiver ran through the ship.

When Bravo whirled a finger and then pointed to a certain instrument on the control grid, Pam returned power.

Bravo took a quick look and just as quickly turned the device back off.

"They're firing off their weapons to try and locate us," he explained. "Trying to locate us with acoustic oscillation, but they don't have anything to blow up that will make a big enough wave."

"What about..." Pam paused her question.

Bravo nodded.

"They should be more careful about attracting attention while in here," he confirmed.

"What are they talking about?" Topeka whispered to Daestar.

"A terror from beyond our universe," Daestar replied in an even lower whisper. Seeing the look of confusion on Topeka's face, she added, "An extra-dimensional entity."

It did not seem to help.

Bravo held a finger to his lips as he passed. He returned a short time later with more food and water for everyone. Topeka gulped her meal down with renewed vigor and then helped Daestar with hers. The next time Bravo brought a meal, Topeka helped Pam with most of hers, too. Only then did she finally ask for directions to the toilet.

"She's going to be okay now," Pam whispered to Bravo, who grew concerned when he returned during Topeka's absence.

When Topeka finally returned, she seemed to notice for the first time the different colors of the gas clouds they were passing through.

"How beautiful."

Bravo smiled, said nothing about being quiet, and gave her a pat on the head before heading off to change places with Lonan once again.

This time Lonan joined them after eating a meal.

"Getting tired of sleeping," he explained. "Wanted some company."

"Shhh!" Pam urged. "Something is happening out there."

The ship's hull rumbled.

"They've found us!" Bravo called out. "Take us deeper into the nebula!"

Pam acquiesced with some grumbling. The Gravedigger surged forward and changed course. The massive dreadnought emerged out of the clouds directly behind them, but the prow did not open.

A grappling hook shot over the Gravedigger's bow.

Missing the target, the line on the hook stretched taut when it reached its limit, and the hook recoiled back, curling the tether into bunches.

Suddenly, the hook's recoil stopped, as though it had struck some invisible wall, and reversed directions—the line became taut once again.

"Pam!" Bravo shouted. "Fire all your port thrusters—now! We're right between them!"

"Between what?" Pam asked as she obliged, but Bravo did not need to answer.

Blue nebula gas began to coalesce, taking the rough shape of a man—forming a body with two legs and two arms, along with a humanlike head where a pair of flaming red eyes smoldered like lava pits. The cloud entity seized the Artomiques' grappling hook and used it to pull itself to the dreadnought.

The Gravedigger shot free before the dreadnought began making several maneuvers to try to free itself from the cloud entity. None of them worked. The vessel was soon engulfed by the cloud—and then the cloud disappeared, seemingly absorbed by the dreadnought.

"Kill all the power," Bravo urged. "Even life support. Let's go full blackout."

The Gravedigger began to tumble, which caused their view of the dreadnought to circle. Daestar watched lights the length of the vessel flicker, flare brilliantly, and then go dark. Soon, the entire ship sat dark and drifted powerlessly.

The dreadnought's main engines abruptly came to life, and the ship disappeared.

Everyone sat silent for a long time before Bravo finally called out.

"Any idea what heading that ship took?"

"Straight out of the nebula," Pam answered, jumping when Bravo suddenly appeared by her on the flight deck. "Damn, but you're fast."

"That turret cannon wasn't going to do us much good against that thing," Bravo replied.

Pam gave the ship's chronometer a concerned look.

"We're running late for our rendezvous."

"Don't worry," Bravo replied. "That hauler is an STS class. Only place Roy could reach is Corsairiana. He'll be waiting."

"That's what I'm worried about," Pam replied. "He's hanging out there in the open—like a sitting duck. He won't be able to run, and he won't be able to hide."

"And that... that *thing* is headed right for him," said Topeka.

Chapter Eighteen:
The Fall of Earth

Daestar felt compassion for Pam when the Gravedigger exited the Nebula and headed for the Lantern Star, only to discover that there was no one there.

The MagLink crackled.

"It's about time," Roy's voice rang out.

Daestar was just as relieved as Pam to discover that Roy Kerk had indeed found a way to hide by parking his heavy hauler so close to the Lantern Star that anyone looking would be blinded. He had stayed on the side away from Corsairiana so as to avoid detection from the planet's automated instruments.

"Follow us out a ways," said Bravo, "and then we'll hook you up to the Gravedigger and take you and your load in tow. Just keep those stars between us and the planet."

He then smiled at Topeka.

"It looks like that *thing* is avoiding anything that can destroy its ride," he said.

"That means Neth is on the loose in our Galaxy," said Daestar.

"Yeah," Bravo replied, "but at least Neth can't spawn since we killed its mate, Nean."

"Maybe," Daestar countered, "but you didn't kill Nean in her universe. If someone else opens another wormhole..."

Bravo's face paled as Daestar allowed her statement to trail off.

"We could be right back to facing extinction," he concluded.

Once the heavy hauler was taken in tow, Roy called over to say he was taking his first sleep in several days and asked not to be disturbed unless there was a new crisis. His voice sounded jittery from all the caffeine pills he had been taking.

As the Gravedigger moved off in the direction of interstellar space, Bravo asked Pam to change course just enough to give them one last look at Corsairiana before they moved too far away.

What the peek revealed surprised everyone except Bravo.

"Where did the Artomiques go?" Lonan called out.

"It's safe to assume that the assault on the Red Citadel failed," said Bravo. "Whip and Rock are probably dead now, but I'd bet money that April girl is still running around."

"Wherever the Artomiques have gone, and

whatever they're doing," said Pam, "we know that they won't be leaving any evidence behind."

"Send out a wide range MagLink alert," said Bravo.

"Are you kidding?" Pam argued. "They'll find us!"

"By the time they trace the signal's source," Bravo replied, "we'll be long gone. Send the signal while we're moving along a different trajectory than what you have planned."

"Here," she pointed to the microphone, "you do the talking."

Bravo thought for a second and then leaned in.

"This is President Bully Bravo, warning everyone to be on the alert for pirate activity that is being coordinated with a new fleet of Artomique dreadnoughts. These ships are lethal and are targeting all Earth military ships. The pirate Red Queen is responsible for the bombing on Ansa. I am attaching the coordinates for her base planet, Corsairiana, to this message. But be aware, the fleet that was guarding Nebula 71 has been destroyed by the Red Queen and her allies. All colonies and Wild Stars planets... take precautions now."

Pam repeated the message through every socket on the MagLink and began changing the Gravedigger's course several times.

"I always heard that your nick-name was 'one-take'," she quipped about the recording having been made on the first try.

"Open up your receiver," Bravo suggested. "Let's see if we can learn what's going on elsewhere."

Countless pleas for help dominated every channel. The Artomique dreadnoughts were wreaking havoc across the entire quadrant, and no ship seemed able to stand against them. Whole planets and colonies were surrendering en masse.

"Looks like we're too late to warn them," Pam observed. "Sorry."

"They're sweeping the stars," said Bravo.

"They claim to represent Earth," said Daestar, causing Pam to angle her antenna.

"All satellite defenses have been disabled and all Earth Forces cleared from the sky," the announcer droned with an unemotional diction. "President Perez and all the leaders of Earth have ceded full control to Achilles Hister and the Artomique Corporation. There are reports that Perez has been asked to stay on in an ambassadorial position. Earth's collapse at home and out in the stars all began when former President Bully Bravo attempted a coup by planting a terrorist bomb at the Ansa peace convention, where..."

Pam shut the broadcast down.

"They'll never believe another word you say," she said. "You're being blamed for everything."

"It's not true, is it?" asked a shell-shocked Topeka.

"He wasn't even there," Daestar replied. "He had nothing to do with it."

"Maybe I didn't start this thing," Bravo growled, "but I'm going to finish it."

"How?" Pam asked. "Right now you're going with us on a ride. Once we deliver that power coupling we can discuss taking you somewhere else."

Bravo's "scary President" face manifested with a fury.

"Don't you realize what's happening?"

"Yes," Pam replied. "And what are you going to do about it? Everything you've done has blown up in your face."

"It was all a setup," Daestar interceded. "They lured me and you to Corsairiana. We were nothing but pawns in a bigger game that the Red Queen and the Artomiques were playing, and we walked right into their trap. We did exactly what they wanted us to do. We blindly started the chain reaction."

Bravo clenched both fists and closed his eyes in an attempt to calm himself.

"Try to relax," said Pam. "Our journey won't take that long. By the time we get to our destination, maybe you'll have a plan."

"Where... exactly... are we headed?" Bravo asked.

"Can't tell you," Pam replied. "You'll understand when we get there. Right now, I need all of you off the flight deck while I chart our course. Again, when we get there, you'll understand why."

Bravo's head was bowed, and his shoulders slumped as he stalked out of the flight deck.

Daestar and Topeka leaned on each other for

support, wincing slightly when the flight deck door slammed behind them and the lock turned.

"What are you going to do?" Daestar asked Bully as she found an unused bunk for Topeka to sleep in, where she instantly passed out.

"I don't know," he replied. "I truly have no idea about what to do next. The Red Queen and the Artomiques have won, and there's no one left to stop them."

"There's still us," Daestar replied.

Bravo sat on his bunk, nodded, and looked at Daestar.

"At least I can still try to help you."

"Why don't you start by telling me about her?" Daestar nodded in Topeka's direction.

When Bravo got to the part of his adventures on Ansa where Erlik made his presence known, Daestar made him repeat the details several times.

"If he selected that time to reinsert himself into the time stream," she said, "then he had to have had knowledge that it would lead to a positive future. I don't understand how he would have accepted this future—or his own death?"

"Something must have changed," said Bravo.

Chapter Nineteen:
All the Gold in the Galaxy

Fully immersed inside the cocoon controlling the Exodus ship, Montchuhasus watched the Gravedigger drop from hyper-light speed a good distance away before beginning its final approach.

Roy and Pam Kerk knew not to make Montchuhasus nervous, as he had been forced to destroy many ships that came to raid the pool of gold that was nearly as massive as his ship, which itself was the size of a small planet.

Seeing that they were not followed, Montchuhasus shut the Exodus's defense systems down and exited the cocoon, joining the immortally beautiful Phaedra to meet the Kerks upon their arrival.

Montchuhasus raised his hand to the hilt of the broadsword slung over his shoulder when the Gravedigger's hatch opened to reveal that the Kerks had brought guests.

Phaedra apparently sensed no ill intent, and placed her hand over Montchuhasus's sword hand to reassure him. Then one of the women they had brought gave him cause for excitement and hope.

"You may have noticed that I'm a god-fearing person," said Pam as she led the way across the landing pad. "Get ready to meet a goddess!"

A statuesque blonde beauty already quite accustomed to displays of adoration, Phaedra did not blush at the compliment. She greeted the newcomers with a smile, introducing herself and Montchuhasus before asking the guests their names.

Pam was looking everywhere except at Montchuhasus and Phaedra.

"Wow," she said. "The place is really coming together. It looks like you've secured all the areas that were relying on magnetic fields. Well done!"

"We already know of you," Bully Bravo said to Phaedra, "but never had the chance to meet you. Daestar and I were with the Ancient Warrior when he saved you from the God Father's prison."

"He's a friend," Montchuhasus reassured Phaedra, who gave Bravo's hand a light shake of greeting.

"Topeka Tanaka," Montchuhasus repeated the name of the one person he had not met before. "Are you from Vu?"

Topeka looked startled and unsure as to how to answer.

"She's from Earth," Daestar interceded. "Her father was a Japanese ambassador, and her mother was from Kansas."

Montchuhasus did his best to hide his disappointment.

Daestar sensed this and said, "I know what it's like, being the last survivor of a genocide. My world was destroyed, too."

Phaedra's eyes flashed a brief moment of jealousy at Daestar's attention, but it passed quickly, her eyes narrowing as she looked inside Daestar.

"I've seen Montchuhasus's memories of you," Phaedra said. "Thank you for assisting with my rescue from the black hole. But you are not the same person as before."

"I've had some trouble with another telepath,"

Daestar replied.

"We were trying to find our way to the Ancient Warrior," Bravo added, "but maybe you can help?"

Phaedra seemed repulsed by the suggestion.

"I do not play games inside the heads of others," she retorted. "It is perverse."

Roy Kerk had been delayed while he dropped the power coupling at the junction between the Exodus ship's main body and the engine section that curved out like a leaf sprouting from a seed. Dozens of workers were there to latch it into place before he headed the heavy hauler to join the others on the landing pad just outside the ship's command tower. Situated at the highest point of elevation, they had a view over the entire ship.

"I see you had better luck this time," said Montchuhasus.

"Most of it bad," Roy replied. "Everything that could go wrong did. But we got the job done."

"Excellent," said Phaedra. "Come inside and relax, enjoy refreshments while you tell us about your adventures."

"Sorry," said Bravo. "But if you can't help Daestar, we need to keep moving."

The petite, middle-aged blonde nodded her agreement.

"They helped us out a lot," Pam encouraged. "We kind of told them that we'd help them with a ship."

"They're not taking my ship," Phaedra asserted.

"No, no," Pam hurried to explain. "But surely we have one to help them."

"They can have the hauler," Roy offered.

Pam cut her eyes at her brother.

"Yeah... that's not even going to get them to the next star."

"There's only one ship around that I see that they can have," Montchuhasus indicated the Gravedigger.

"Wait a minute," Roy started to argue.

"We owe them," Pam interceded as Lonan nodded his agreement.

"But that's my baby," Roy pleaded to no avail.

Pam handed a control chip to Bravo.

"Be kind to the 7557," she said. "She's a good ship. Bring her back safe, if you can."

Bravo looked at Topeka, whose attention was locked on the massive pool of gold tethered to the ship by a long, cylindrical mechanical arm.

"Are you staying?" he asked.

She nodded, seemingly oblivious of the words.

"That's got to be all the gold in the galaxy," she murmured in fascination.

As the pair returned to the Gravedigger, Montchuhasus could hear Bravo talking to Daestar, and had to smile.

"I don't care how good a shot Montchuhasus is, if anyone learns where all that gold is, they'll be attacked in more waves than he can shoot down."

As observant as Bravo considered himself, he never noticed how Topeka turned and watched with envy as he walked away with Daestar.

Once the Gravedigger had powered away and moved into hyper-light speed, Phaedra nodded to Montchuhasus.

"Time to call the fleet back."

Hundreds of vessels of every shape and size quickly filled the space all around the Exodus and the gold field. Many of the ships were old, but all of them were outfitted with state-of-the-art equipment procured by the Kerks.

"Once the Exodus engine is finally working," he said to Phaedra, "we'll be mobile and no longer vulnerable."

"Then we can finally move to the next phase," she replied.

Chapter Twenty:
The Fall of New Atlantis

Even with the Gravedigger's engines at full burn, it took six months for the vessel to leave the galactic plane and pierce the wall of hot plasma that surrounded the galaxy like the inner membrane of an egg.

It had been a harrowing journey, as Daestar watched despair creep into Bravo's face as he listened to the unending reports of the Artomiques' unstoppable rampage across the stars.

There were no longer any Wild Stars or colonies of Earth—or even an Earth for that matter. There was only the Artomique Empire, ruled over by the young

Achilles Hister and his mate, Nefarimor, the Red Queen.

Stories about the atrocities they committed while solidifying their control filled the MagLink channels.

Bravo quit listening when he learned that a statue had been erected on Earth, proclaiming him a hero who had sacrificed himself to free the galaxy of the scourge of immortals and pave the way for the Artomique Empire.

"That's even worse than what they were calling me before."

Finally, the planet called New Atlantis, which mirrored the same course as the Earth far below in the galactic plane, came into view. It was at that same moment Bravo realized that they were being followed.

"It's the Artomiques," he growled.

"How could they find us?" Daestar asked.

"It's my fault," Bravo replied. "I used our transponder to lead the Earth fleet to Corsairiana. The Artomiques must have intercepted that message."

As they neared the planet, they saw waves of ships evacuating from spaceports all across the planet. Bravo took the controls and steered the Gravedigger away from the crowded sky lanes.

"I think I remember the way from the last time we were here." He guided the ship down to a marble-pillared building that stood higher than any other on the planet and landed on the small platform next to it, where a lone scout ship sat.

A man dressed in Wild Stars armor appeared from behind one of the columns, headed in the direction of the scout ship. He paused, giving Daestar and Bully a look of curiosity.

Daestar, too, felt a mystery about the middle-aged man, but she could not place him. It was a frustrating thing for her, no longer having the ability to pluck answers from others.

"Daestar?" he asked tentatively.

"Yes," she replied.

He took a startled step backwards.

"I thought everyone left behind in this galaxy when we journeyed to the horseshoe galaxy was dead and turned dust. Twenty years for us was supposed to be two hundred for you! How is it possible that you're still alive?" Then he hesitated as a realization swept over his face. "I'm sorry, you must be her descendant by the same name."

"No," Daestar answered, "I'm the same woman. I just took a different shortcut into the future."

"You were there," he pointed a finger of confirmation, "the day the Ancient Warrior flew his skier into the past and immediately returned, bringing a Rogue planet along in tow."

Daestar nodded as she solved the mystery of the man's identity. What had once been long red hair worn in braids was now a short cropped haircut that was turning white at the temples.

"Redrick?" she hazarded a guess.

The man nodded with a smile.

"Where's the Ancient Warrior?" Bravo asked.

Redrick gave Bravo a long look but quickly determined that they had never met before. He turned his attention back to Daestar.

"He's the same place he was the last time I saw you," Redrick nodded his head back the way he had come, "sitting on his skier in the pool. Only, I don't think he's planning another trip in time. Ever since he heard the news about Erlik's death, his melancholy has dragged him down to a level I've never seen before. I didn't have any trouble getting him to issue an evacuation order after that Artomique fleet was discovered headed our way ..."

"Fleet?" asked Bravo. "It's not just a ship?"

"It looks like all of them," Redrick replied. "And after what that fleet did to all the other Wild Stars, evacuation was the only choice. The Wild Starriors were decimated after their battles with the Purple Order, and we've never had a chance to rebuild."

"Abandoning an indefensible position is sometimes the only option," Bravo conceded.

"That's just it," said Redrick. "The Ancient Warrior is staying behind, alone. I think he intends to do the same thing he did with the Brothan fleet, when he destroyed their fleet with that decoy rogue planet."

"I don't see another rogue planet," Daestar whipped her head around, scanning the sky.

"There isn't one," said Bravo. "We would have

seen it when we arrived."

Redrick nodded.

"The Ancient Warrior is going to draw them in close and take that fleet down with him."

"No!" Daestar exclaimed.

Redrick thumbed in the direction of the shadowed interior.

"I've tried my best," he started walking again for scout ship. "But I've got family that I need to protect. There's no one else left in this galaxy who can help."

Stunned, Daestar watched the scout ship quickly lift off and join the thinning stream of ships heading into the sky. The city below and the whole world around them in every direction was eerily silent. It was the quiet of a tomb.

They found the Ancient Warrior inside, sitting atop his skier as it floated toward them across the shimmering pool, but he was unaware of their presence, his head down and lost in thought.

Bereft of her telepathic skills, Daestar found the Ancient Warrior's behavior an impenetrable mystery. She was baffled at how he could sit and wait to die, taking all of New Atlantis with him.

In the skies, even the straggler ships began to thin as the evacuation was nearly complete.

"Are there no more mysteries left for you to solve?" Daestar called out, flailing for anything that might break the Ancient Warrior's depression. "You've moved whole worlds from one galaxy to another and back again. That's an incredible thing! Are there no more accomplishments or challenges you'd like to face?"

"The Great Machine," he muttered as he looked up, his eyes showing only the slightest hint of recognition.

"Yes? What about it?"

"When we crossed the voids," he mused, his eyelids raising slightly, "there were structures there. Had to go around them."

"Around what?"

"I never thought about that before..."

"Thought about what?" Daestar pressed.

"Where my ancestors disappeared to. I've always looked in other galaxies—so many of them. Found

Phaedra and other descendants like myself. But never found our ancestors. Never found my parents."

Daestar could see that he was slowly rousing, albeit ever so slightly.

"I always tried to avoid the gas structures that make their own highways between galaxies. I never looked inside one of them."

"There's still time," Daestar prodded.

"We're out of time," Bravo growled. "That fleet of Artomique dreadnoughts will be here any time now. Daestar, you know how much faster they are than the Gravedigger."

"The Brothan once did the same thing," said the Ancient Warrior.

"I heard it didn't turn out so well for them," said Bravo.

The Ancient Warrior shook his head.

"They destroyed New Atlantis."

Daestar and Bravo each looked around and then back at each other.

"I changed time," the Ancient Warrior noticed their confusion. "Saved New Atlantis and destroyed them. Saved your Earth at the same time."

"Okay," Bravo stretched out the word. "Do you have to wait until New Atlantis is destroyed again before doing something to save it?"

"I will finally die with this world. That's why I sent everyone away."

Daestar was frustrated and beginning to feel agitated with her inability to make a difference.

"There's another choice," she said before she even knew what words would come next. "It's just you, us, and the world. Why not take on a new quest?"

"A quest?" the Ancient Warrior asked.

"Solve that one big mystery you've never solved," she replied. "What happened to your ancestors? Where are your parents? Why did they abandon you and Phaedra?"

"I probably knew once and forgot."

"Oh, no, you didn't. I shared your memories, remember? I've seen glimpses of your youth that you seem to have forgotten. Massive oceans where men rode water bikes like the one you built to travel back in time with—when we first met. You remembered how to build that; why are you denying to yourself those other memories."

"Phaedra," he answered.

"That wasn't you," Daestar ventured. "Your obsession with Phaedra was something the Five-Thousand Fingered Hand kindled in you. They thought they could control you by distracting you. But you surprised them. Instead of becoming lost in melancholy over lost love—you went and looked for her! Searched across the galaxies and aeons for her—until you found her. It just didn't work out like you hoped. But that wasn't your fault."

The Ancient Warrior's eyelids raised slightly further as he turned his head to look at Daestar.

"Your wife who was a telepath..." she started to say.

"Our children were all monsters," the Ancient Warrior turned his head away as his chin began to fall to his chest. "I had to destroy my own children!"

"For the sake of the galaxy!" Daestar urged. "The galaxy still needs you. You can't let the Artomiques destroy everything you've ever built. They're not even from our reality. They're creations of time manipulations by the Brothan—your ancient enemies."

The Ancient Warrior took a deep breath and shifted in his chair. He leveled his gaze at Daestar.

"Like she was, you are one of the Five-Thousand Fingered Hand."

"Yes," Daestar confessed. "And still you trusted me with your memories, with a message for your son. Why?"

"I saw your soul."

"Did you not see the soul of your wife?"

"Love is blind," the Ancient Warrior sighed. "What would you have me do?"

"You've got a mystery," she said. "Giant structures hidden between the galaxies—and your missing ancestors. Don't you want to know if there's a connection? It's something you've overlooked. And by taking one last quest, you'll also deny your enemies the victory they desperately need. Keep them chasing you, and they won't have time to inflict misery on your galaxy. Because, you know, when they do, they'll make the God Father look benevolent."

The Ancient Warrior ground his molars at the God Father's mention.

"From what I understand," Bravo ventured back into the conversation, "the God Father could possibly still be alive. You know his revenge will be terrible. You're the only person who can stop him. And help Daestar."

"Help?"

"Yes," Bravo pressed, "the Hand took her telepathic skills away. Damn near killed her!"

The Ancient Warrior slowly stood, leaned across the water and reached a hand to place a palm on Daestar's forehead.

"That will not stand."

"Meaning?" Daestar asked.

"I will start the planetary engines."

Daestar shook her head when Bravo's inquiring face indicated his hope that she might have been healed.

The Ancient Warrior shifted in his seat, causing the water skier to create ripples that spanned out across the pool's surface. For a moment, Daestar's heart skipped a beat, having once watched him ride into a waterspout to travel back in time. But this time, there was no whirling vortex to whip him away in time after he worked the instruments between the handlebars.

He briefly fired the planetary engines, causing Daestar and Bravo to stagger as the world shifted beneath their feet. Then he shut down both the engines and the planetary satellites that provided light.

New Atlantis went dark.

"Think this will evade the Artomiques?" Bravo asked.

"They'll never know which direction to look," said the Ancient Warrior. Then the instruments on the skier began emitting a repeating beep.

"Someone on New Atlantis is sending out a signal," he explained, turning a glare first at Bravo and then Daestar. "It's coming from here."

"That would be me," Bullson stepped out from behind a column, proudly displaying a transmitter beacon.

"Son," said Bravo, "what happened to you? Last

I saw, you'd just taken down the rogue service droid and were facing off with the Artomiques."

"Sorry, Mister President," Bullson said in a tone neither Daestar nor Bravo had ever heard from him before. "I wanted to come see you earlier, but Achilles wouldn't let me. You did everything he wanted you to do. Sent the Earth forces right into his trap. He said you'd lead us wherever he wanted to go, and you have."

Bravo's "scary President" face was back.

"I knew something had happened to you," he said, "when you didn't show up to help in the fight with the pirates on Corsairiana. I was worried about you."

"I've found a better way than yours."

"He's been corrupted," said the Ancient Warrior.

Daestar gasped when Bullson tossed the beacon to one side and drew the massive blade that he carried in a scabbard attached to his back.

When he drew the sword, it glistened with turquoise blue light.

"That's a Toridian sword," said Bravo.

Even the Ancient Warrior took notice enough to leave his skier and step onto the pool's edge so he could take a closer look.

"Montchuhasus gave that to Erlik to safeguard," said Daestar. "You stole it!"

"That means," Bravo hesitated before uttering his next words, "you... you knew what was about to happen on Ansa."

Bullson smiled. It was not a pleasant smile, but more of a twisted gloat. He then hefted his blade up in preparation to strike and, in the same motion, launched himself with blinding speed at his father.

As well trained in military combat as Bravo was, even he could not react fast enough to defend himself. But the Ancient Warrior could.

A single punch, thrown with seemingly casual effort, knocked Bullson sprawling and unconscious. But before Bravo could thank him, the Ancient Warrior's knees sagged as though injured. He slipped weakly back into the seat of his skier.

"What's wrong?" Daestar asked.

"I've had to do this too many times before," he said. "Kill a child who has gone mad. So many of my

children went rogue and had to be put down—and I was always the only one who could do it. There is a pain from having your hands washed in the blood of your own children—a pain that nothing can erase. Now, my one child who gave me hope has also been taken away. I think dying with New Atlantis is the best idea."

A new signal on the skier instruments gave another warning.

"In fact, they're almost here."

"Do we have to die as well?" asked Bravo. "There's no way Daestar and I can escape in the ship we arrived in. Do you really want to watch your son's wife, the love of his life, die in front of you?"

The Ancient Warrior let out a deep sigh.

"The Artomiques are too close now for tricks." He nodded his head for them to join him on his skier. "Get on board."

Daestar quickly sat on his lap, but Bravo stopped to pick up the Toridian blade.

"No way I'm letting him keep this," he grumbled as he pulled the scabbard, sheathed the blade, and slung it over his shoulder. He then placed his feet on one of the skier's pontoons and took a good grip. The Ancient Warrior threw the engines into full throttle and shot off the pool's surface and into the air, passing between the Parthenon's marble columns and into the air, headed toward a lone Wild Stars scout ship parked not far away.

"What about Bullson?" Daestar asked.

"What about him?" Bravo asked grimly in return, drawing a look of disconsolation from the Ancient Warrior. "He picked his side."

"That's what I once thought," said the Ancient Warrior as they landed next to the scout ship, his hand lingering on the handlebar as he hesitated to leave the skier. "Now, I blame those who poisoned them more than their victims."

Bravo stopped at the ship's hatchway.

"He'll be fine," said the Ancient Warrior, ushering them both inside. "Calm your heart, and we'll soon be too far away for him to find you again. With his skills, the Artomiques won't destroy New Atlantis until he has been recovered."

The Ancient Warrior gave his skier a last look of

farewell, and followed them in. When he launched, he did not wait for his passengers to strap in. Soon, both Daestar and Bravo were floating in the weightlessness of space, neither being fitted with gravity boots and the scout ship unencumbered by gravity plates.

Daestar was surprised to see New Atlantis fire up her planetary engines, and launch on a similar course behind them.

"See that?" The Ancient Warrior pointed forward, where a stretch of darkness revealed one of the massive structures of gas stretching from Earth to the other galaxies sprinkled like brilliant, sparkling jewels against a background of black velvet.

He steered around the cloud, allowing New Atlantis to continue directly into the gas. There, it exploded, creating an even more colossal explosion—on a scale of star nova.

In the brilliance of the flash, their tiny Wild Stars scout ship changed directions and finally escaped detection into the void.

"Roy and Pam won't be happy about the loss of the Gravedigger," said Bravo.

"They can afford a new ship," Daestar replied.

"Did that blast get the fleet?" Bravo asked.

The Ancient Warrior shook his head.

"They must have turned back at the last minute," he said. "It's like someone warned them."

"Bullson," Bravo's voice was filled with disappointment and rage.

"That means the Artomiques are still in control of the galaxy?" Daestar stated as much as asked.

"They won, again," said Bravo.

There was a long interlude of silence before Daestar spoke next.

"And... ?"

"And, what?" asked Bravo.

"There's something more bothering you," she said.

"With so many time travelers at our disposal; Erlik, his daughter, Mack; how could we come to this?"

"Surprise is a time traveler's weakness. They're vulnerable to the unexpected. I'd say that there was

hope, since Mack and Akara left with Atlanta, right before the explosion."

"They did?" Bravo perked with a glint of hope that quickly faded. "Then why haven't they interceded?"

"They couldn't have gone far before the blast. I was hoping that maybe one of them had some sort of intuition—but if they had, we would have heard from them by now. They must have been caught in the blast."

"I was thinking the same thing about Bullson, until he showed up and proved something even worse had happened to him."

"What about Bully Shawnee?" Daestar asked.

"Since we've gotten to the point where we're at," said Bravo, "we can only assume that something unexpected happened to him, too, probably because of something my son did."

Epilogue One:
The Long Journey
Previously

Tall Trees Wolf was chattering away when Bully Shawnee rejoined her, stepping through the hatchway from the rear compartment. She could quickly see that he had no idea what she was talking about.

She calmed herself for a moment before speaking again.

"Where did you go?" she demanded, refusing to look at him when he took the seat next to her. "Where's Bullson?"

Shawnee hesitated to answer.

"I know you. You've been traveling in time again. And right in the middle of our conversation?"

Shawnee nodded his concession.

"Bullson probably won't be coming back," he confessed. "He needed my help to stop a Saturnian-Eybontic hybrid that was on his way to kill his father, Bully Bravo."

Tall Trees blinked.

"Your namesake?" she confirmed more than asked. "Well, of course you needed to save your uncle. Sorry if I sounded a little miffed."

Nothing more was said for some time while she

piloted the Wild Stars scout ship away from Ansa and headed for the upper plate of the galactic plane.

"I'm sorry," Shawnee finally broke the silence. "I won't do it again. It's not fair for you to be trapped here while I travel about. For the rest of this journey, I'm only going to be here with you."

"For a minute there," she laughed, "I thought you'd been off with another woman." She felt more carefree, reassured that the trip would just be the two of them, instead of three.

Shawnee shifted uncomfortably in his seat.

"Well," said Tall Trees, "if you do go somewhere else, at least next time—take me with you?"

"Can't," Shawnee replied. After one look at Tall Trees' facial reaction, he quickly added, "You're my anchor here. If we both left, I'd never find this ship again."

"This is going to take a while," Tall Trees raised an eyebrow, still refusing to look in his direction. "To save Earth, first we've got to find an arm of the Great Machine that still works, and then use it to corral that black hole, Ruin. After we used it to defeat the God Father, it was headed away into the intergalactic void, where it's going to be awfully hard to find. Then we position Ruin so that Earth's sun will have its natural orbital wobble back while it cruises up and down the galactic plane."

"I understand. The God Father did a good job of wrecking our galaxy."

"That's what revenge-crazed people do. At least he, and all of his Purple Order, are dead now." She let out a sigh of relief.

"Regardless of how long the job takes," said Shawnee. "Turn the MagLink off. I'm not going anywhere else. I'm here with you, for the whole long journey."

Tall Trees finally turned to look Shawnee full-on in the eyes.

"Your face!" she exclaimed. "The scars are gone. You're gorgeous! I mean... you were always an attractive man, despite them ... but now, wow."

Epilogue Two:
Arrival of the Grimgrip
Artomique Ice Tower—Pluto

Achilles dodged easily when the Red Queen threw the 17th-century Qing-dynasty vase with the arm motion and violence of a professional baseball pitcher. The vase struck the ice wall, and the shattered pieces of elaborately decorated porcelain scattered across the white marble floor. Some pieces disappeared into the tiny ring of ground-hugging mist where the heated floor touched the Plutonian ice.

"Those damn Grimgrip!" She was incensed. "Earth was warned about them, which means that you should have known. Now we're being attacked all along our frontier that borders the great void. We didn't get even a single moment to enjoy our victory before we were locked in another war with an enemy that my Hand knows nothing about!"

"We'll deal with these Grimgrip the same as we've dealt with everyone that came before them," said Achilles calmly, "and everyone who comes after them."

The Red Queen stormed angrily out of the room.

Shaking off the many psychic needles that had embedded across his mental shields, Achilles knelt and examined the painted side of some of the larger pieces of porcelain.

A shadow fell across the doorway where the Red Queen had just exited.

"Would you like some help with that?" asked a white-haired man who looked like he had seen better days. His was the tortured expression of someone dealing with a horror that he struggled every day to internalize but could neither speak about nor forget.

"The plan went well, old man," said Achilles.

"Call me God Father."

"Father of what? This is something new."

The white-haired man's body movement showed a hint of irritability when he replied.

"I've never told you before, but I am the God Father of a whole galaxy."

"What are you, Wild Stars?" Achilles tried not to tense up. "Why did you help me?"

The God Father's irritation spread to his eyes.

"No. The departed Wild Stars were my enemy, the same as you. I pledged to show you how to take control of these insignificant flickers of light away from them, and have I not delivered?"

"You have," Achilles replied. "You trained me well in the skills of telepathy. Even while the Red Queen was transferring my consciousness into this new body, she was unable to discern all my plans. She could not crack the crystal mind shields you taught me to build, and I came through complete and without encumbrance."

"You have a unique mind," said the God Father. "Once, I had a legion of followers with minds like yours. Have you ever thought about bleaching your hair white—like mine?"

Epilogue Three:
Phaedra's Army
Location: Unknown

Montchuhasus was falling forever, grasping futilely at the spiraling tendrils of gas clouds that whipped past, but could find nothing of substance to seize and stop his fall. The brilliant light below him grew so strong that he could not shut it out from his eyes as the increasing pressure on his chest began to crush him.

"Wake up!"

Phaedra's voice became a lifeline that drew him slowly out of his nightmare.

"What's wrong?" she asked.

Montchuhasus jumped out of their bed and shook his head, looking wildly around to confirm that he was indeed awake, and the reality he had just experienced was the dream. He slapped his foot twice on the floor to confirm it was solid.

"I was back at the quasar cluster," he explained, "where we recovered this ship. But this time, I was adrift in space, alone, without the use of the Great Machine."

"You've traveled many millennia back and forth in time." Phaedra extended a hand to draw him back to bed. "It's no wonder you're having feelings of being alone and overwhelmed."

"Yes," he conceded as he sat down.

"Maybe that will change tomorrow. Now that this ship is fully maneuverable, we can finally travel to Akara's World. These Brudwata, they are descendants of your friend's tribe?"

"They have to be the children of the Broadwaters."

"Then they will become the vanguard of my new army."

Final Epilogue:
A Time Dilation
Earth
2005-2020

Deep within the Earth, where even the shallowest of breaths required herculean effort, Kearston clutched Carlton MacKanaly's arm as they were ushered through a hallway of amber.

With the oppressive heat pulling the sweat from her body, she was glad to be only wearing a one-piece swimsuit and ran her fingers along the wall of amber as they passed, wondering if it might be melting.

Her action seemed to anger the fishmen escorting them, as a sharp-edged spear swept up and down in the space between her hand and the wall.

Then they emerged into a massive cavern that had been carved out of more amber or some similar mineral, and was lit by glowing rocks of phosphorus.

In the center of the chamber slumbered a monster the size of a whale.

With the clawed arms of a saltwater crocodile, but many times more massive, the creature uncoiled and roused like a waking dragon, but there were no wings—only a tail. Neither did its mouth spout fire, but its face and eyes were almost human.

Those eyes latched onto Kearston and Carlton.

"You will be my emissaries," said the creature.

"I didn't see its mouth move," Carlton whispered.

"I am Vishnatay."

Kearston looked behind her and saw that all the fishmen had prostrated themselves on the floor.

"Now would be a good time to run," Carlton suggested.

Kearston shook her head.

One of the fishmen with eyestalks stood and began to speak in English.

"Without the power of the Marzanti trident," the creature had difficulty forming some of the words, "it has taken us uncountable ages to dig only a few small holes with access back to the surface. Now, all the

Isshla are running out of time."

"Why?" asked Kearston. "What's changed?"

"Nothing has changed. What we Isshla always knew would happen has happened. You ugly, hairless mammals have poisoned the whole world like you poison everything. We once declared war on your kind and nearly eradicated you from the planet, but something went wrong at the end. The Marzanti trident somehow released all the energy we had built into our machineries that were designed to flip the planet's shifting mantle. Your continents would have been turned upside down and the world cleansed for population by the Isshla and the next wave of Marzanti. This world would have become the ultimate world of the Marzanti."

"I take it that you've given up on that plan."

Kearston kept shaking her head to keep Carlton from asking any questions.

"Without a Marzanti trident, there is no chance. It has taken us this long just to scratch a few access points to the surface waters. But the explorers we send out rarely return, and we're running out of time—because the surface poison has seeped so deep into the Earth's mantle, that it's beginning to affect the water in the realms of the Isshla."

"Are you declaring war on the surface world again?"

"Right now, our only focus is on escaping the prison that was once our home—before we are destroyed along with it."

"I understand," she replied. "How can we help?"

"Help? I know who you are," said Vishnatay through the fishman. "You who read minds has a mind with much to read of your own. A survivor of a destroyed world. Your people who once colonized the stars to escape the Isshla have found new enemies there. You still mourn the loss of a sister in that holocaust. Now, I give you a message that all humans should mourn when they hear it. I am reawakened. The Isshla have labored long and hard to undo the damage done to our world so many millennia ago. But now the great world machines are repaired. Tell the hairless monkeys that one day, soon, they shall again fear the water."

"Which is it?" Carlton could contain his curiosity no longer. "You want to escape? Or you want to declare war?"

The stalk-eyed fishman made no further comment, waving with his spear for them to leave.

"Be glad that he didn't answer that," she whispered, but was more worried about her own unasked question: *Define soon?*

She had the impression that the timetable was based on how long it took for the entity known as Vishnatay to become fully roused from his long sleep in his chamber of amber.

They were herded back into another cart on a rail, but this time they were being elevated. Several stops were made of several hours each, at spots where fresh water pooled near rows of mushrooms.

"Think these will take us on a trip?" Carlton asked.

"I think we're already down the rabbit hole," Kearston answered with a thought she plucked out of the back of his head.

He smiled, thinking that they thought alike.

After several more days, they staggered, lead-legged, out of the smoking rift of a volcanic island and discovered that they were in the middle of another ocean, lost and alone, surrounded by an endless sunset vista of clouds, islands, and water.

Then Carlton saw a fishing boat in the lagoon below, and they ran down the mountainside, shouting and waving their arms. It seemed they were too late; the ship had unfurled its canvas and turned its prow toward the open sea.

At the last second, a sharp-eyed deckhand working the fishing nets spotted them and the ship turned around.

Night had fully fallen when the ship once again set a course for the open sea, but this time it carried two additional passengers.

Still dressed in their swim gear, they were given shirts to wear by the crew, but Carlton's frame was so much larger than theirs that he could not attach a single button in the front.

Left alone at the crew's dinner table and surrounded by fresh plates of fish and jugs of fresh water, Carlton looked at Kearston and shook his head.

"We're on the other side of the world," he determined. "How did those men understand you?"

"I may not speak Chinese," Kearston batted her eyelashes, "but I seem to have expressive eyes."

"For a minute there, I believed what Vishnatay said about how you could talk inside people's heads."

"Did you look at the calendar on the wall?" she asked.

"I can't read Chinese," he replied.

"Maybe, but you understand numbers?"

Carlton did a double take when he read the date of 2020.

"That can't be right," he protested. "We couldn't have been gone longer than a few weeks!"

Kearston stayed quiet, letting him sort his thoughts on what seemed like an impossible situation. It took some time before he came to his own realization of a seemingly impossible fact, but the moment he grasped it, Kearston was confounded by his first thought.

I missed my class reunion!

"What was that all about?" he finally asked. "There is no way that we can tell anyone about anything we've experienced—not without being locked up in a mental institution."

"You know," she deflected, "after what we've been through, there's something I should tell you."

"What's that?" asked Carlton.

"My name isn't Kearston. Well, it is if you consider it to be the Americanized version. Or Earth-adjusted might be a more accurate explanation."

"I think there are a lot of things you should explain to me."

"My real name is Kearstar. My family always has ... had ... the surname of Star. Our homeworld, Vahn, was destroyed by Brothan. Now, I'm the last of my line."

"You're saying that you come from another world—which was destroyed?" Carlton asked. "Now I think that *I'm* being adjusted."

"Remember what I said before... about the Wild Stars?"

His body language was that of ignorance, mixed with impatience from having to wait for an answer. In his mind, she caught the mysterious phrase; *I'm waiting for the other shoe to drop.* Then she caught an image of a person sleeping on one side of a wall, listening to the springs of a bed groaning on the other side where a person had sat down and dropped one shoe, but the other never fell.

"Your whole life has been affected by the Wild Stars," she said. "I think it's time someone finally told you what is really going on, both here on Earth and out there," she pointed to the portal where the night sky, unpolluted by city lights, showed a rich canopy of flickering pinpricks of light, "beyond the stars."

He knitted his eyebrows in confusion.

"I'm about to drop the other shoe on your whole world."

The Birth of the Wild Stars (A Foreword Afterward)

After learning how to spell my first two words, Stop and Go, I immediately drew a crude comic strip about military tanks crossing rivers and hills. I've been writing, drawing, inking, and coloring stories ever since.

Scripting everything from non-fiction to multiple fiction genres, there was one particular subject that I kept returning to: creating a unified multiverse where all the adventures were interconnected. Having watched the first moon landing broadcast live, I wondered what it would be like as mankind spread out into the stars in the manner that European settlers once explored the western United States. This stellar migration would likely be far wilder than the Wild West ever was, giving me the description for my concept. The Wild Stars delineates a section of the Milky Way galaxy, but the stories expand far beyond that.

My first tale of the Wild Stars was the very last chapter: Final Conqueror. I was 13 when I submitted it to Warren Magazines in hopes of making a sale, and while it was accepted, it was not for pay. They chopped and edited it down into one long sentence to fit into a corner of the Fan Fiction page of the January 1972 issue of *Eerie* Magazine #37, which was later reprinted in Dark Horse's Eerie Archives Volume 8 in August 2011.

The unabridged version of Final Conqueror did see print in the summer 1977 issue of the fanzine Ecstasy Oblivion #2, for which I also provided the cover and other interior art. But that cover was not connected to the story.

In 1977, the Ecstasy Oblivion cover did appear in my The Multiversal Scribe magazine with the story it illustrates, "The Boundaries of Decision," which unfortunately carried the typo title of "Boundries." I created all the content for TMS, and when the printer went bankrupt this was the last print job they produced. Because of that urgency, when I finally got the tapes from the typesetters (it was a whole different world of preparation back then), I pasted the entire magazine's layout in one sleepless night and delivered it the next morning. There was no opportunity for type corrections.

My second published Wild Stars story also had a serious presentation flaw, but it was not as bad as the first. "The Boundaries of Decisions" is reprinted with the corrected title for the first time here, including the original art with a few modern enhancements. The story's location, Trovador, is mentioned in Wild Stars 3: Time Warmageddon as a frontier city where the future President Bully Bravo's boots laid the first footprints.

But "The Boundaries of Decision" was far from being the second story written. The year before The Multiversal Scribe collection of artwork and five stores in five genres was assembled, in 1976 I was submitting my novel Wild Stars Rising (different from Wild Stars 4: Wild Star Rising) to New York publishing houses. Sometime afterwards, I read an article about upcoming movies in Starlog Magazine. It mentioned one named Star Wars. I was worried the title was a little too close to Wild Stars, but I had no idea who George Lucas was and thought it would be quickly forgotten after release. Another movie discussed was Damnation Alley starring George Peppard and Jan-Michael Vincent. Being an adaptation of a novel by Roger Zelazny, I figured Damnation Alley would be the movie people remembered from that page. I got my predictions reversed.

I continued to pour my time into developing the Wild Stars, with my next novel being Wild Stars 6: Orphan of the Shadowy Moons that is currently being serialized in the 2022 issues of Cirsova Magazine of Thrilling Adventure and Daring Suspense. Unlike my other novels written during this time, I never submitted Orphan to any publishing house, and although some elements, like the controlling of massive machines from a distance with a tablet, have gone from fiction to fact in the 45 years since, none of the core ideas have shown up in other places.

In 1984, I went back to doing things myself and began adapting another 1970s Wild Stars novel, First Marker, into comic books. The 1988 Volume 2 #1 issue was not only created, written, lettered, penciled, and inked by the same person, I also printed it in my garage on a Chief 17 press. Like the foil stamped front cover, and die cut front and back covers, these were all comic industry firsts. I even took it a step further and used a printer's technique to fade a mountain in the background on one page throughout the print run. If you have a copy with a solid mountain, it comes from the front of the run, and the more it fades, the later. This made each copy an individual art print.

My April 1998 limited edition novel, Under the Wild Stars, was adapted into the 2001/2002 Volume 3 series of comics that completed the graphic novel Wild Stars 1: The Book of Circles—Recalibrated. To share a couple of hidden threads, Volume One was presented in the form of a football game. It begins with a pre-game discussion, starts with a whistle, ends with a gunshot by a man wearing a striped shirt, and then goes into a sudden death overtime. It could also have been titled Time Travel Twice Told, because it tells the story in long form, and then repeats the concept in short form in the "overtime" conclusion.

Also in the 1990s, I decided to try the submission process again, and once again began seeing concepts show up elsewhere. When I was submitting the short story that would become the comic book section of Wild Stars 2: Force Majeure, I told the editors to think about the cannon fire in the climax of the 1812 Overture when reading the part about the water geysers exploding around the vehicle on the Prairie Bay plain of Mars. The next year, there was a commercial about a new car driving through a barren plain as geysers exploded all around it, accompanied by cannon fire and the 1812 Overture. Sure, coincidences can and will happen, but that was pretty exact. There were instances of movies with dozens of identical plot points lined up in a sequential row. In one case, I searched the credits for the writer—and after looking up a name I did not recognize, read his statement on the web about how he got the idea from something he read somewhere but didn't remember where.

A similar experience happened to the previously unpublished story included here.

"A Templar Knight on the Roof of the World: Bees with Nuclear Stingers" was submitted with no luck to a long list of magazines. I always got nice letters of encouragement and compliments back, but no sale. Then an element from the story, which hinges on lost VHS video footage being found, became a hit concept in Hollywood. I shelved the story and stopped doing submissions until I met Cirsova Publisher P. Alexander.

As you might have already guessed, I work on the entirety of the Wild Stars at the same time (the conclusion of this 12 volume series is already plotted), establishing milestone markers and filling the gaps between. Volume Five has reached the point where both "Boundaries of Decision" and "Bees with Nuclear Stingers" take place. There is a thread between them, hidden like the subliminal design structures in Volume One, where you will find a teaser for "Bees" on page 262 with pencils by Dave Simons and gray-tones by me.

Still to this day, I keep adding artistic embellishments to my Stops and Gos.

Bees With Nuclear Stingers:
A Templar Knight
On the Roof of the World

Lying flat on his back and gazing into a clear evening sky, Saltian Rock was startled when the calm night exploded in a thundering shower of incandescent light. A crowd of voices cheered at once when he turned to the beautiful woman by his side. The opening pyrotechnics of the 1998 Fourth of July summer festival filled the sky and the reflections that shimmered across the river that bordered the park.

A firm believer in karma, Saltian thought it was strange when Sierra commented, "Wouldn't it be great if one of your ancestors had invented gunpowder? And then got a patent on it!"

"I wouldn't want to be responsible for the death that followed." Saltian concentrated on the lights sparkling in her eyes, which suddenly turned sad.

"Tell me, Old Salt," Sierra asked at the precise moment when, over her shoulder, Saltian noticed the county sheriff walking through the blanketed crowd, with eyes focused on him, "have you ever heard any news about your son?"

"I'm more worried every day." Saltian smiled at the realization of how well she knew him. "Haven't heard from him since he went off chasing abominable snowmen ... again."

The sheriff towered over Saltian and Sierra, silhouetted by the fireworks that framed his shoulders as he demanded; "Saltian Rock, come with me." He added, "This concerns your son."

Saltian was up.

"He must have found one this time!" Sierra shouted optimistically as she caught the truck keys.

In the parking lot, Saltian groused with the sheriff over the reason for the brisk pace with which they walked to the patrol car. He demanded to know what news he had about his son.

Hours later, Saltian was still waiting for answers when he landed by jet in Maryland.

At Andrews Air Force base, a pair of military police were waiting in a green sedan. No one spoke during the one hour ride across the Virginia State line.

They entered Arlington and approached the section of the Pentagon where nightshift laborers toiled beneath huge lights.

Triple holiday overtime. Saltian distracted himself with calculating workman's wages, ignoring the fact that his heart felt like a vigorously strummed guitar.

There was an elevator entrance where six marines stood guard. Through the windows of the intact original Pentagon wall, Saltian could see that the inside of the entire structure had been ripped away and was being replaced with massive new steel structures that burrowed deep underground.

Dressed in distinct blue uniforms, trimmed with brilliant white, the Marines conducted Saltian below and down a marble hallway that glistened with fresh polish. He was the only one ducking the low ceiling as they approached a wide pair of doors marked 'Conference Room.'

The Marines waited outside as Saltian stepped inside and onto the upper level of a vast, empty, amphitheater. The room was illuminated by several spotlights aimed at a single chair on a raised center stage floor. Walking down through the rows of stadium seats, he heard a door creak behind the stage.

A tall, attractive woman with long dark hair and Native American features stepped into view. She was the first unarmed person he had seen since leaving the city park.

"Hello." She spotted Saltian instantly. "Stay there. I'll join you."

"What's happening here?" Saltian extended his hands with the palms out. "I'm flat confused. Do you know something about my son?"

"I can answer your questions." Her footsteps echoed up the stairs. "First, Mister Rock, my name is Rose Stone."

"You're Stone and I'm Rock." Saltian shook her hand. "Are we related?"

"Maybe." She had an easing smile. "Sit. Talk with me. Let's discuss your son."

"Just tell me. Is he all right?"

"There has been some serious trouble," she replied, "but he is uninjured."

Saltian worried that her statement held ominous overtones.

"The military found him yesterday on an island south of Pakistan. History says that island is haunted by the dead and no one has set foot on since the time of Alexander the Great."

"I don't understand." Saltian wanted to ask what the military was doing there. But he was perplexed by how comfortable he felt in this strange woman's company, despite his certainty that events were about to turn very bad. Something about Rose Stone's presence and innate confidence communicated with Saltian on subconscious levels. Either that or he was having another of those crazy impulses that always kept getting him into trouble with pretty women. "Would you mind running that one by me again?"

"You have six questions," said Rose Stone. "Who? What? Where? When? How? And the most important question of all. Why? These are same six questions that I have. Perhaps we can work together. Help each other."

"Then how about answering the 'who' for me. Who are you?"

"I'm a consultant; an advisor on matters that include the spiritual." Rose Stone handed him a pen and a clipboard that held a single document. "First, read and sign this. It's a Mandated Federal Secrets Affidavit. You will never repeat anything you are about to witness under penalty of treason. The punishment for violation of this agreement is immediate, covert execution. Do you understand?"

"No. In my whole life, I've never heard of anybody outside of the Secret Service being asked to sign such a thing. Why do you want it?"

"It's not for me. This is so that you can sit at the meeting about to be convened. This concerns your son."

Saltian was stunned.

She looked him in the eye.

"Weren't you disappointed with your training as a triathlete for the 1980 Olympics?"

"Until the President canceled..." Saltian started to lament about the U.S. boycott of the Olympics that year, then thought deeper. "I'm picking up what you're laying down." He signed the document without reading a word.

"I hope you can help me to understand your son and his actions." Rose Stone tossed the clipboard onto the next seat. "I met with him this morning and he said something that made me wonder..."

She was interrupted by doors opening everywhere at once. The action was so on queue with his signature that Saltian instinctively looked around for spying eyes.

A number of men in suits and military dress uniforms grouped together on the lower levels. The marines that had escorted him now each guarded a different door.

Saltian forgot about them. He focused on the lone man who approached the chair spotlighted in the center of the stage floor. When he passed through the lower row of men surrounding the stage, Saltian felt disturbed. The politicians were bad enough, but he immediately disliked the uniformed officers. It bothered him every time a braggart flashed every medal as though his chest was a trophy case. Saltian knew it was not a rational reaction, but he had seen too many medals awarded posthumously on The Wall engraved with the names of those who died in Vietnam.

The youngest man in a suit sat with the generals for only a moment before noticing Rose Stone and Saltian.

"Saltian Rock," said Rose, "I'd like to introduce you to Senator John 'Hoot' Gabrial. He is one of Washington's unsung rising stars. One of those dreamers of new programs."

The senator shook Saltian's hand. "Mister Rock, the reason we asked you here is because…" the senator was animated with excitement that Saltian could not understand, "Rose wanted you here. But I have some questions before we get started."

Saltian finally made eye contact with his son.

Jaw set square, Jock Maloney confidently met his father's eyes and nodded once.

Saltian recognized the fading red blemishes on Jock's face. They were cartridge-ejection burn marks caused by the rapid firing of an M16 rifle.

The senator cleared his throat.

"Sir, have you ever known your son to lie?"

"Never."

"So, you're saying that if your son told you that he'd seen a UFO, you'd believe him?"

"Definitely. Especially something outlandish like that."

"Why?"

"He was never taken to rash actions or statements."

"Never? You're certain?"

"Look, if my son said he saw a UFO, then he probably took a ride on it just to be sure. And he'd find a way to do it. Believe me, I know. I raised that kid."

The senator and Rose Stone exchanged enigmatic glances.

"Let's get to it then, shall we?" When Senator Gabrial returned to his chair he nodded to the military man seated to his right.

"Thank you, senator," the officer stated loudly as he grudgingly freed his concentration from the contents of a thick file folder. As he stood, lights flashed from the multitude of medals clustered across his chest. "Jock Maloney," he turned his attention to the center stage, "my name is Brigadier General Rogers. While this is an informal proceeding, as a former member of the United States Air Force, you understand the importance of discretion in all matters discussed here?"

Jock nodded.

Saltian felt the muscles in his jaw flex as he clenched his teeth.

"Good. Then let's start with the facts," the general held the folder aloft, waving it above his head in a counterclockwise direction, "in reverse order. It seems to me like that's the only way we'll be able to sort any of this out."

When Saltian again began to scan the room, Rose Stone indicated with a nod that he should concentrate his attention on the stage.

"Jock Maloney, you were found on a desert island off the coast of Pakistan," the general looked straight at Saltian, "where a remote control RASA unit was being covertly installed."

Rose Stone leaned close to Saltian's ear. "Radionuclide Aerosol Sampler Analyzer. A radiation detector. It can identify signs of nuclear explosions."

"You appeared out of nowhere," said the General Rogers. "And you say that … you swam there?"

"Yes."

"You swam ten miles through shark infested waters? And you did this after crossing the mountainous northern border of India and Pakistan, then traversing tiger filled jungles? All on foot and alone?"

"Yes."

"So, while I assume that you were able to accomplish these incredible feats thanks to your SERE training, at some point you became aware of the news that the CIA had been caught flat-footed with India's nuclear testing feud with Pakistan. While Pakistan conducted a retaliatory test, you broke into India's nuclear facilities and downloaded all their internal files to a friend of yours via the internet."

"Sir." Jock shook his head. "Not the heart of their nuclear commission. Just a remote office with a network link."

"And, via this network link, your friend covered your movements with help from the other hackers who claimed credit for what they purported to be a prank."

Jock sat like a statue, his expression chiseled.

"I'll quote the record. Shortly after that was when you miraculously appeared on a legendary Island of the Dead, scaring the hell out of the RASA installation crew and..."

Saltian noticed that Rose Stone had smiled at some hidden joke when the general referred to the pilot SERE training, which he knew meant; Survive - Evade - Resist - Escape.

Rose Stone looked him in the eye and seemed to read his mind. "Spelling aside, I prefer to think of the word seer as referring to a giver of divine wisdom. Tell me about your son's beliefs."

"I never thought the boy had it in him," Saltian intentionally detoured. Despite his earlier braggadocio, he was astonished that Jock had been involved with the recent events that had quieted the nuclear feud between India and Pakistan. Astonished, but somehow never surprised.

"You did not answer my question," Rose Stone pressed.

"Do religious beliefs even matter anymore?" Saltian stalled. "All routes supposedly lead to truth. Some of us just travel the path least taken. Believe me when I tell you, some people get real upset when you say something that they don't agree with."

"This is very important." Rose Stone paused a single breath. "I'm going to tell you something, and I don't want you to waste time asking questions. Your son has been involved in the deaths of several people. One was a religious man."

Saltian did not think or react. He just blurted it out. "I raised him to be a Templar Knight."

"I didn't realize the Order was still active." The perplexed expression did not seem to fit on Rose Stone's face. "I've only heard that term used in modern times as a ceremonial honor for Freemasons or in reference to ancestral descendants who claim to guard the Ark of the Covenant."

"Take my word on it, I'm not old blood. And I'm not a Shriner."

"Are you Christian? Protestant? Muslim? Jewish? Buddhist? Hindu? Or something else?"

"All of those, and a little of something else," Saltian replied.

"Atheist?"

"I raised Jock to understand all religions and to accept each person for themselves and not their beliefs, or lack thereof. I wanted him to always make up his own mind and not be influenced by the desires of others."

"Then you contradict yourself." She shook her head. "You just said that you raised him to be a Templar Knight. You influenced him yourself."

"No." Saltian watched as the general paced in circles around Jock, asking who he had talked to since his rescue on the island. "No, I taught him to be a complete individual and realize that in the search for truth sometimes you must first dispel misconceptions. When he was old enough to start making choices for himself, I quit teaching. I let him go into the world and figure it out for himself. But these days, the more I think about it, I think Jock always kind of worried that his old man might be suffering from post-traumatic stress. Shell shock."

"I don't understand. That sounds more like the mantra of science than of religion. What higher calling does a Templar Knight serve?"

Saltian decided to recite his treatise on religion. "All religions share uncountable common themes, which all sprouted from teachings that originally were, like Gandhi in modern times, about understanding of the world and the pursuit of peaceful coexistence. I believe that the Romans who executed Jesus of Nazareth later decided to use his words as a form of mass control. Even later still, they added the doctrine to oppose all men until there was no other god. This came back to haunt them when Mohammed added that same doctrine to Islam."

Rose Stone made no reaction, sitting with rapt attention to Saltian's words.

"But there are teachings that have been forgotten, thought lost for two-thousand years. The Dead Sea Scrolls tell how the Romans persecuted and extinguished the Order of Jewish healers who had trained this Jesus during his supposedly unknown years. I believe that it was the original Roman architects of the Catholic theology who claimed that

Mary Magdalene was a whore and that Jesus' youth was lost. None of the gospels said that. I feel certain that they knew. All illustrations of him are of his youthful appearance, not the balding middle-aged man who was crucified. Even before the scrolls were rediscovered, the Templars taught that Mary was the wife of Jesus, and the mother of his children."

"You don't have many Catholic friends, do you?" Rose Stone observed. "Several hundred million people might be insulted by what you just said. What about the fellowship and sense of community that churches develop?"

"Wait, wait, wait. I'm just trying to explain what separates a Templar Knight from the guarantees that other religions make based on the promise for the hope of salvation. People today are not aware of the whole truth. Just like in the days of ancient Rome, religion is used as a tool by men with their own agendas. Some agendas are better than others, but I always worried about religions that were taught exclusively by men. What would a female priest be called? A priestess?"

"Why not a shamaness?" Rose seemed uncomfortable with what she heard. "You learned this from the Order of the Knights Templar?"

"Exactly."

"So Templar Knights believe that all religions are empty faiths?"

"No. No. If wearing blinders makes someone happy then that's fine with me. A Templar Knight serves a purpose other than that of promises. I was describing the difference between their society and mine. I'm not attacking them. However, they did attack us. There is a reason why you haven't heard of us. While the Order was founded under the claim to protect European travelers to the Middle Eastern Holy Land, the truth is that a clandestine inner circle protected wisdom like that of the Dead Sea scrolls and other great knowledge. When the Roman Church learned this, there was a holy war like never seen before or since. After inquisitors heard the testimony of Phillip the Fair, a bankrupt King of France who failed his testing for admittance, the Templar Knights were burned at the stake for heresy. Only after they thought us extinct were we able to continue our work."

"How did Phillip fail his test?"

Saltian hesitated.

"The last time someone talked about that, a lot of people died."

Rose sat mute, still waiting for an answer.

"The final test was a demand to spit on the Holy Scriptures. If you did, you failed. I'm sure Phillip told the Pope a different version of that."

"Where are you organized today?"

"No church except the earth and the sky," Saltian gestured below and above, "and gatherings of three or more. Our hearts are our temples. I was first recruited into the Order while serving in Nam."

"Is that when you changed your name? Is Rock a common name within your order?"

"I became a shepherd to all who walk the path to universal co-existence, dedicated to promoting the common wealth of wisdom. But, some knowledge has to be held secret to keep from being lost forever."

Rose Stone's eyes widened. "That explains a lot."

"You mean that I confirmed what you already knew? You work for the government. This isn't exactly the first time that I've had... what's the best way to put it? ...difficulties because of my personal religious beliefs."

"Honesty is always refreshing." Rose nodded her head, but her eyes were distant. "Three out of four people only say what they think you want to hear."

Saltian saw her indecision. "Look, I know what I believe isn't popular. But consider history. The Aztecs and Mayans are perfect examples of uncompromising religions that ultimately destroyed their own civilizations. Compare that against the backdrop of the plague ridden Dark Ages when early Europe was totally in the grip of ignorance mandated by the Church. The end result was different only because the Knights Templar were there, working in the shadows. We saved the knowledge of things like architecture. Renegades from our order later founded the secret organization of stone masons that has flourished in modern times. I don't mean any of this negatively. Nothing personal."

"Quite a concept. A very isolated concept." Rose

Stone turned her attention to the words of Brigadier General Rogers, then whispered, "Personally, I believe that World War Two was the prophecied Armageddon and that the world around us now is the golden age."

Saltian wondered if Rose Stone was telling him that she was beyond the fear taught by many religions.

"Enough of your exploits in Pakistan and India," the general declared to Jock Maloney. "We should discuss the events that occurred prior to that. I have a videotape supplied by the Chinese government which shows the burning of a sacred temple and... murder. Dead Americans!"

At the mention of a burning temple, Saltian remembered a late April newspaper article about the Takstang Monastery, a sacred Buddhist shrine that had been destroyed by a mysterious fire. He read the article because his son was in Bhutan. The Monastery had been located on a twenty five hundred foot cliff overlooking a road that ran north to the twenty five thousand foot peaks that comprised the Himalayas. China sat on the other side of the roof of the world. The fire had been blamed on the butter lamp of the caretaker Buddhist monk. He was missing and presumed dead.

Sniffing cigarette smoke that wafted through the air, Saltian recalled his mental visualization of a snow-covered mountain cliff where a wooden temple was engulfed in flames.

A wall-sized screen descended from the vaulted ceiling as the lights dimmed. Footage of snow leopards stalking wild goats was fast forwarded through until the image appeared of a robe adorned Buddhist monk inside an ornately decorated room. He sat cross-legged on a wooden floor in front of a hanging Mandala tapestry, which Saltian knew Buddhists believed served as a focal point to draw the karmic wind from an extinct universe. As the monk chanted, religious wheels were spinning everywhere. Bells hidden in silk flags were ringing, while several columns of incense smoke filled the air. Oddly out of place in their western clothes and gear, members of what Saltian supposed to be the documentary crew were sitting behind the priest, all imitating his posture and chanting in unison with him.

The events that followed were so swift and brutal that Saltian's mind refused to comprehend them. After the screen went blank, he sat dumfounded and confused, trying unsuccessfully to recall what he had just seen.

The tape was rewound and replayed in slow motion.

Chinese soldiers entered through a wooden doorway at the same moment that the Mandala tapestry and the monk exploded into flames. Even with the slow motion replay, Saltian could not tell the cause of the blast, only the source. A subsequent wall of fire swept through the temple's interior like a wave, rolling over every thing and every person. The images ended abruptly.

"Spontaneous combustion?" Brigadier General Rogers mused as the lights returned. "Or a can of gas and a match? This was the second time you had been enlisted as pilot by that documentary film crew we just watched die. Two years ago you were the first foreigners permitted into the Shennongjia National Park in China. This time you went to Bhutan on the Chinese border of Tibet. The Land of the Thunder Dragon. How come you're the only one who survived a visit to an unarmed farming community?"

Saltian could tell that his son was devastated by what he had seen. Jock took a deep breath and released it as audibly as possible.

"Do you want the truth?"

"Nothing but."

"I was releasing a Yeti that the film crew had captured," Jock stated to roused mumbling. "I made a pact with the Buddhist monk. While he distracted the others, I set the Yeti free."

The general's jaw dropped the maximum distance possible. "A Yeti? An abominable snowman? A hairy leftover from the neanderthals? He didn't happen to be riding on a unicorn?"

There were muffled laughs.

"A Yeti," Jock confirmed. "Two feet taller than me and covered in golden-brown hair. He was intelligent." Jock looked dead on into the general's baleful stare when he added, "There was more awareness in those eyes than I see in most people."

The general's back stiffened at the rebuff.

Saltian restrained the grin that tugged at his cheeks. He recognized the flash in his son's eyes.

"I agreed with the monk that the Yeti should not be caged to use in medical experiments," Jock said. "I'd just learned from the team leader that capturing a Yeti was the secret purpose of the expedition. That's why the Artomique Corporation financed it. The monk spoke about personal sacrifice and the penalties dealt for disrupting what he called the universal harmonic balance. I thought he was talking about me, until I saw the fire from a distance. After that, the cost of not going to India outweighed the cost of going."

"You contend that what we just witnessed was in fact spontaneous combustion?"

"I never knew what happened until just now. I was following the Yeti out, making sure it would be all right. When the Yeti stopped and turned, that's when I saw the temple burning from a distance. By the time I looked for the Yeti again, all I found were the tracks that led me safely across the mountains and into India."

Saltian noticed that Jock's demeanor toward the general had changed. While still cordial, Jock was like his father and not inclined to accommodate the antics of fools.

The general's posture was one of outrage. "Why would a religious man go to such great lengths? Why are there dead Americans?"

"I imagine it was because of the Chinese."

There was another rumble of low laughter as someone said, "He imagines, all right."

"Why would you think that?" asked the general. "What could possibly justify their deaths?"

"I'm not justifying anything. I'm just explaining. On the first expedition to Shennongjia, I heard rumors that the Chinese had offered a reward for a captured Yeti. On this trip, when I returned from a supply run to Bangkok, the airport authorities at Paro impounded the plane because of news that a Megare, that's what they call the wildmen, had been captured. They consider the Megare to be holy. They blamed me. I was lucky just to reach the Monastery

when I did. Then the Chinese showed up. Only drastic action secured the Yeti's freedom. Sir!" Jock concluded with emphatic courtesy.

"Incredible." Brigadier General Rogers shook his head and looked at Senator Gabrial. "It seems incredible to me that you could think anyone would believe any of this! We have all the evidence right here for ourselves; a dead Buddhist monk, a dead American film crew, and dead Chinese soldiers! And all of this happened at China's doorstep, with the original copy of that recording in the hands of the Chinese government! And by your own admission you conspired with this monk to kill the others."

"I never said that. You're changing my words. I was rendering humanitarian aid at the behest of a local religious leader. I did not kill anyone. If I were now on active duty, I'd have to ask: is this a preliminary hearing for a court-martial?"

"Are you wondering what the punishment is for a war crime?" The general smiled. "Despite the improbability of multiple spontaneous combustion, maybe I could give you some benefit of a doubt if... if at some time you had informed the American consulate in Bhutan."

"There's not one."

"If you had tried to inform someone, anyone! But, no! No." The general circled Jock, leaning closer as he spoke. "You were just getting started. You had to mosey on over into the next two countries and stir up the bees there as well. And let me point out, we're talking about bees with nuclear stingers! On that tape I saw snow cats, but I didn't see any snow men. And you claim that a snow man acted as your guide to India! Preposterous."

There was a silence where the only sounds were the general's pacing footsteps.

"It was you." Brigadier General Rogers glared at Jock. "You were responsible for this catastrophe. Why did you do it?"

At those words, Saltian Rock looked around and evaluated the improbability of personally rescuing his son. The way events were unfolding, he considered it unlikely that he might ever again be so close. There was electricity in his pulse, and those old, crazy impulses were definitely back.

"I did nothing wrong." Jock's back became rigid. "I did exchange gunfire with Chinese scouts, but I did not kill anyone. I fulfilled a promise."

"And you say this Buddhist monk, this temple caretaker, asked you to go to Pakistan and India?"

"He was a seer. He had been plagued by visions of massive destruction caused by a nuclear exchange between those two countries. Then he had a vision where he shot an arrow between two warriors who raised swords against one another. One was startled and the other found satisfaction in laughter. "

Again, Rose Stone smiled at the word 'seer.'

"You're telling me that a bald hermit living on a mountain top knew what was going on between India and Pakistan before even the CIA did? And you were his symbolic arrow?"

"Yipper."

"What?"

"Yes, sir."

"That's it!" Brigadier General Rogers threw his hands up so emphatically that he lost his grip on the file folder. It spun for several feet and then crashed in a shower of scattered paper and clips. Even though he spoke softly, his curse words echoed.

"Thank you, General." Senator Gabrial stood and looked directly at Rose Stone.

She nodded once.

The senator cleared his throat. "Gentlemen, that concludes this meeting. Jock Maloney, you and I will talk shortly. Good day."

Everyone started for the exits. Jock Maloney glanced at the papers on the floor as two Marines escorted him out the same door Rose Stone had entered through.

"You misspelled Shennongjia," he told the general.

"Is my son under arrest?" Saltian put his hand on Rose Stone's shoulder. "I heard what they just said in that deposition. International espionage. Death. Destruction. I'm sure that our government, along with China, Bhutan, India and Pakistan—all of them—they all want my boy dead."

When Rose Stone nodded her head, he tried to read her expression.

"You thought this was a judicial hearing?" she asked. "I'm sorry. Let's start over. You've been completely honest with me, and I should do the same with you. My full name is Rosetta Stonewolf. I am the last shamaness of the KaNze, the tribe of the South Wind, better known as Kansas. You commented earlier about male-dominated religions. My people always chose spiritual leaders regardless of gender. Just as you took a name in honor of Jewish warriors who were massacred by Roman soldiers, my tribal name came from the custom of naming every shaman as a wolf, with the balance of their name being an emphasis on their special gifts. My gift is the deciphering of language, words, and intent; the spirit. The senator considers that to be an unusual political asset."

"So your name is Rosetta Stonewolf." Saltian waited for the bad news. "That doesn't answer my question. Is Jock under arrest?"

"This was never a trial. This was a job interview. I plan to recommend to Senator Gabrial that your son be offered the position as head of the newly established Extraordinary Patents Office. This special assignment required special attention to the screening process."

"The what?" Saltian tried to mentally gauge his own reaction, but could only think of words like *flabbergasted* and *discombobulated*. "I've never heard of the... the what?"

"And you should tell no one about it. Remember the paper you signed. Given your religious beliefs, that should come natural for you." Rosetta's expression was serious. "Consider this—if someone came up with the concept of time travel, or another fantastic invention, what would happen next?"

"They'd patent it?" Saltian thought about Sierra's earlier stray comment during the fireworks display and wondered why remembering her made him feel guilty.

"They would, hoping to achieve permanent control. Now you get into the complicated twist of things dealing with potent and dangerous concepts. National security, the military, sometimes even religion, all get involved. Thank you for your son, Mister Saltian Rock. I can't think of anyone else in the world better suited for this unbelievably complicated and challenging job than Jock Maloney. His handling of extraordinary events in Asia may have averted a nuclear armageddon that would have destroyed one fifth of the planet's population. He answered to a higher calling and never lost his center of personal justification. That tells me he has all the unique qualifications that this job requires."

"That didn't sound like a job interview to me." Saltian realized that he was losing his chiseled face. He fought the smile with gritted teeth. "Hey... would a Templar Knight be eligible for consideration?"

When Rosetta Stonewolf stood, her grin was almost eerie. "I suggested that the senator consider your son. The original plan called for the agency to be administrated by a think tank that Brigadier General Rogers is the head of."

"Not that strutting...?" Saltian thumbed toward the center floor.

"Hoot feels that think groups ultimately reflect only the views of the leaders."

"Isn't the government just a really big think tank?"

"Hoot must have agreed with your assessment of the General. It was Hoot's idea to have one candidate interview the other. In retrospect, I agree. It provided a unique perspective on the attitudes of each man."

"So what was that business with the video recording?"

"Chinese soldiers raiding a temple in the last surviving Buddhist nation? It's interesting that that particular holy site, like a phoenix, has been destroyed and reborn many times. Legend says that it was the spot where the Guru Rinpoche arrived riding on a fantastic winged tiger and introduced Buddhism to the mountains."

"It's history," said Saltian. "The tape, I mean. No one's ever going to see that again, are they? The Chinese probably don't even know you have it."

Rosetta Stonewolf's pretense of a mysterious smile had none. "There might be rumors, legends. Who knows how the truth will be twisted?"

"That's what I've been talking about." Saltian had to ask, "One more thing," otherwise he knew he would wrestle with it forever. "And I figure you owe me since you tricked me."

"Tricked you? How?"

"I never would have told you about the Knights if I didn't think my son's life was in danger. Don't argue the point. You asked me here because of something Jock said. What? What was it?"

"You raised your son to pursue peace." Rosetta Stonewolf rolled her head. "Then you encouraged him to train as a warrior and join the military?"

"Hey, everyone agrees that even Jesus knocked over a few tables. And when he was young ..." Saltian imitated Rose Stone's mysterious smile. "I taught Jock to be well balanced. In retrospect, I think he was more interested in learning how to fly."

Rosetta paused. "I asked Jock one question. Already knowing the how, I asked him why he did what he did while in Asia. He replied that the monk had told him that he must become enlightened, for the sake of all living things."

"That's what I always taught him! The great truth is not about promises! The creed of a Templar Knight is the willingness to sacrifice yourself for others."

"Your son is a modern day Charlemagne." Rosetta nodded her confirmation.

"Thank you." Saltian knew that his broad smile confessed his every emotion. "That's a better nickname than what I got stuck with back in Nam. Everyone always called me Don Quixote."

"All fervor aside," Rosetta's hand casually brushed across Saltian's back, shivering his spine with the refreshing chill of an early spring breeze, "your son has learned the key common denominator of all spirituality—that enlightenment is achieved through inner calm and confidence. Then you change the world."

"My son is fine." The relief in Saltian's back felt as though he had just dropped a railroad timber off his shoulders. "That's all I ever prayed for."

On the following page, a scene from Wild Stars: The Book of Circles where the events of this story were first referenced.

The Boundaries of Decision

Chapter One
Trovador

"A place of iridescent beauty upon a crystalline landscape."

No words better described the picturesque structure of Trovador. The sleek, streamlined city rose proudly on the interior slope of a massive dead volcano. Visitors arriving by space liner often looked on in amazement at this perfect society nestled in the snow-covered panorama of this dead planet.

From the spaceport on the rim of the volcano, new arrivals were ferried free of charge by skier freight in a circular motion down in to the city. Flight was not permitted, and the slopes were too slippery to climb. It was thus that Trovador retained her fashionable richness, for the return trip to the space port was an astronomical fee—one that only the wealthy could afford.

It is a fact that Trovador's spires were considered to be the brightest in the galaxy, and her shadows the darkest.

There were few places on any planet where a human being could sink lower than the ground slums of this city on Fenton IV. The streets stank with the filth that filled the air and seemed to grasp the inhabitants and pulled them down into the muck. The lower-level buildings rarely housed a scrupulous soul. It was a melting pot for countless races from the stars, filled with hate, violence, and prejudice.

Jeanne Filaire was the perfect example of fallen grace and dignity as she shuffled down the dark alleyways, her long coat dragging. Deep inside, she held precious the moments of the life she had led before trapping herself here. Her beauty and touch were still with her, as she was far from old, but they were little more than a shell for the hollow woman who had once sacrificed her feelings and personality for prettier things.

The son of a diplomat had drawn her away from the realities of life, charming her with the company of world leaders and the supposed organizers of truth and unity. They had toasted drinks by the barrel to her loveliness, and she believed she had been raised upon a pedestal different from all those who had preceded her. But dreams are often a lie, and she was discarded when they were through.

It was hard for her to accept the truth of what she had been used for, hard to throw away the dreams of velvet perfection they had offered her. It was harder still to be a lone woman abandoned in Trovador.

The stalkers of the alleyways had eventually accepted this humble beauty who walked the streets like a lost soul. There were men who admired her face from a distance, but were too repressed to approach. Still, their attention kept the wolves away.

It no longer mattered to Jeanne what happened to her body and soul, as she worked from day to day as a pretty in dingy barrooms, earning a simple living. There were no more shiny tomorrows for her, only the false fantasies of yesterday for as long as she was trapped on Trovador. There were ways out, but they demanded that she lower herself even farther. Deep inside she knew it was a price she would have to pay, even when she had nothing left to give.

That was why when the clangor of a vicious street fight reached her ears, she did not turn and run like a sensible person. Instead she sought out the struggle, fearful that one of the few friendly people she had met might be in need, and friends were a rare gem to her.

Her soft footfalls gave no sound as, like another shadow, she found the end of a blocked alley. Her breath caught when she saw four crumpled figures lying face down in the gloom, scarlet pools widening around their shoulders. Their clothing was like nothing she recognized, and the backs of their heads were reptilian in nature. These were strange aliens from reaches she had never heard, and for the first time she felt fear that she had involved herself in affairs that were none of her concern.

She was startled to realize that someone stood only a short distance to her side, staring at her through the dark. She whirled to face him, defiant, but careful not to say a word as she challenged him with her eyes.

"Jeanne?" His voice was almost a whisper as he took a hesitant step toward her. "Jeanne Filaire?"

Jeanne saw that he held his left arm clasped tightly to his side, as though protecting some savage wound, while firmly clutching a large sack beneath his right. She feared that this was some thief who haunted this artificial jungle, who had seen her in a bar and would be asking her for aid she might be unable to refuse.

He sagged to his knees as air hissed between his teeth. Jeanne grabbed his shoulders and helped him back to his feet. A normal human like her, the lines of his face were creased with worry and not entirely unhandsome. It took her a moment to think of how he might look without those lines, and she was shocked when a realization came to her.

"James Forester? My God! What happened to you?"

He gave a grateful smile when she said his name.

"I was wondering something of the same about you, lovely lady." His voice was still the same, filled with warmth and friendliness. "I'm sorry as hell that we're both here. Forgive me."

Before Jeanne could inquire what it was he wanted, a light flared from the open end of the alley, and a blast struck Forester full in the head. Like a robot with its power source severed, he collapsed to the filthy pavement.

Jeanne was dumbstruck. Insider her weary breast she felt her heart beating with emotion, the first true feelings she had known for ages. She looked with fear at the approaching figure, his gun slowly lowered.

"I'm surprised to see you here, Jeanne," said the District Officer Conrock as he stepped into the light. He was not known to be a good man, but sometimes watched with care over his selected sheep, one of which was Jeanne. It was well known that he had a great weakness for ladies who had fallen to misfortune, which rumor had due to some tragic episode in his past. But this was outweighed by his reputation for ruthlessness.

"He's not dead," Conrock announced when he saw the consternation in her eyes. "I only stunned him. What happened here? Who are these dead men?"

"I don't know." She knelt and caressed Forester's face. "I arrived just before you."

"Do you know him?"

"From my past."

Conrock examined the other bodies with dutiful disinterest. Plucking a transmitter from his side, he dialed a code and plugged the receiver in his ear.

"Street Crew? I've got a cleanup in the Thirty-fourth District, ground level. There are four expired Reavers from the Black Star system in a dead end alley. Yes. The ones I told you to expect. I'm doing a follow-up, so clear me through Central. Thanks."

Conrock picked up the sack Forester had been carrying, glanced inside, and grimaced. He attached it to a clip on his belt and then lifted the unconscious man over his shoulder.

"What's going on, Conrock?" Jeanne asked timidly. "What are you going to do with him?"

"I have no choice. I can deposit him at Central, where most likely he'll never be heard of again. Or, I can ask you to volunteer your home for the necessary follow-up investigation. That is, if you'll allow this murderer into your home?"

This was not at all like Conrock. Jeanne had often heard how he executed rapists and murderers in the streets without qualm. She could not fathom his interest in James, or her.

"Follow me," she decided that she was unwilling to sacrifice Forester to certain doom. Trovador has become filled to overflowing with undesirables lately, and the rumors of sanctioned liquidations filled the streets. The Unification movement started by the Artomiques had encompassed Fenton IV and cleared martial law for them.

"What do you know of this man?" Conrock asked as he followed her in the direction of the apartment blocks.

"Nothing recent. He was a friend when we were both youngsters at the Career Training Institute on Earth. He was determined to become a Forward Scout for the Space Corps, wanted to see the awe and wonders of the galaxy. But we were nothing more than good friends when I quit the Institute to walk on the silver skyways." Just saying the word 'friend' gave her heart a flutter.

Conrock caught her arm as they passed beneath a street globe, where they could each see the other far too clearly.

"What *kind* of man was he?" Conrock asked.

"A proud one, filled with ambition. I don't understand how he came to ... this."

"I can," Conrock muttered then fell silent.

Nothing more was said as Jeanne led the way to the sixth floor apartment that capped a thriving nightclub and restaurant. The noise from the repetitive beat of the music droned constantly, day and night.

Conrock dropped Forester onto her dilapidated couch, almost with gentleness.

"Why are you doing this?" Jeanne opened Forester's shirt to reveal a jagged gash along his ribs. Wetting a tablecloth, she laid it across the injury.

"Why are you?" Conrock countered.

"I'm not sure. I don't know if he's still the same person I knew. That really doesn't matter. I'm not the same person I used to be. I guess I just need friend."

"I can't think of a better reason, not in this city. Your friend was lucky, that gash was from a laser. If he'd been shot with a scatter gun like the Reavers usually carry, he would have lost his whole side. Obviously they couldn't sneak them through customs, and lasers are all you'll find on the black market. Can I trouble you for a drink?"

Jeanne poured a glass of wine as she watched Conrock place the sack Forester had carried at the foot of the couch and detach some intricate circuitry from his belt pack. With precision he placed it at key points on Forester's face.

Conrock thanked her for the drink and downed it in a single gulp.

"There are many methods of interrogation, but I like this one best. All I do is ask the unconscious subject my questions in what I assume to be chronological order, and they remember them like a dream. It's usually like listening to the poor singing

in the street, begging to scrape up their exit fee from Trovador. Are you interested in hearing the story about how he came into that alley tonight?"

"Very," she confessed.

"Then help me select my questions. What he answers will determine his punishment. Unfortunately, there is no such thing as a pardon for murder in Trovador. The only choice is in how the punishment is delivered."

Conrock's behavior seemed peculiar to Jeanne. If he had already determined that Forester was guilty, her only hope was to plead some kind of mercy in how he was executed.

Chapter Two
The Private Memories of James Forester

I've been damned! The entire universe has plotted against me and sabotaged me at every conceivable turn of my life!

It was easy in the beginning to plan, as I stared up at the stars, so vast and deep, offering untold mysteries and wonderful discoveries. So much of our galaxy is still untouched, even as we now proudly proclaim ourselves masters of this eternal realm. I've striven my whole life for the opportunity to plunge into that deep, black ocean and plumb her depths.

I hurried through my days at the Career Training Institute, determined to set a new standard in everything I did. What I should have done was pay more attention to all those impressive women. Why didn't I spend more time with that beautiful Jeanne Filaire? She was like smooth zephyr on a hot summer day. But I wouldn't let myself get distracted. My eyes were on the stars.

I made Second Division Forward Scout for the Space Corps right out of the Institute. The counselors told me how that outfit would fulfill my dreams, and satisfy my memories when I was torn from duty by old age. I would have signed away my entire life if I had been allowed. Fortunately for me, that wasn't an option—at the time.

I quickly learned that being a Forward Scout is nothing more than a life of endless loneliness, paving the way for those who come later. There is no excitement in plotting the courses of the stars and providing all the data that determines the tracking courses of Star Cruisers. I served for years on the same vessel, never rising in rank or touching a single planet. Any adventure we did encounter was quickly turned over to Trotter Class Cruisers.

Sure, they gave me some great mind tapes to play in my dreams, but daily life was as empty as the void and as grey as the ship's metal. They don't even provide scout ships with the sections of transparent titanium that composes major sections of Star Cruisers because they don't worry about us suffering any phobias. We're too hand-picked.

When my commanding officer handed me my renewal papers, I promptly zapped them in a matter transformer. Apparently, that was not appreciated. It was appreciated even less when I told my C. O. what I really thought about the whole zig, and I found myself dumped at the nearest port.

So there I was, stuck at the spaceport on Fenton IV, trying to collect my back pay. You never bother collecting it when you're on active duty because you never leave the ship. That's when I was informed that I'd have to travel back to my point of origin to collect from the local office. The problem was that they'd left me with no travel vouchers. I'd have to earn my way back home, which meant that I'd mostly like die of old age first.

That was when I fell for the free ferry ride to the glittering city just below the volcano rim. I figured, why not? It might give me some opportunities for work.

No one told me about the ferry fee back out until after I'd arrived in Trovador. The people here really take advantage by forcing people to work for subsistence wages that don't quite cover your basic expenses. It's a trap you can never get out of.

A job as an enforcer for a city official was the best pay I could find. The work was beyond humiliating, because it made me into a part of the institutional victimization of the innocent. Probably because of my pent up anger from how my military service had ended, I made a big noise of it when I finally walked out. It certainly wasn't the best way that I could have handled things, but it made me feel better at the time. Took my last paycheck and headed for the lower levels.

I actually earned more at the ground level than I ever could have in the towers, and I enjoyed providing protection for local shop-owners. Cracking the heads of thugs made for good therapy, but I was still subsisting more than existing.

That was when I first saw *her* at the street bazaar. There was some sort of festival going on for some trivial excuse to throw a celebration, and the most beautiful woman I have ever seen was standing close to the flap of a makeshift cutlery stand, as if she were trying to melt into it. Her face was almost indescribable--her complexion as white as fresh fallen snow, and the pores of her skin filled with flashing gems, some tiny and some large. It was the best bejazzling that I had ever seen, with the gems seeming to be a part of her perfect body that was wrapped in a tight-fitting gown that glittered more than Trovador's uppermost spires. It was obvious that she was no Earth girl, because what I first thought was an elaborate cape was actually exquisitely plumed wings attached to her back. But what really caught my attention was her eyes--they were large, wide, and filled with a fear that seemed to emanate from her core.

Now, everyone on the ground levels of Trovador is in some sort of distress. And everyone is looking for something to make them forget about that pain. I'm no different. After one look at her, I suddenly realized just how lonely I had been for so long.

I started to approach her but hesitated when I saw how the local District Officer was hovering around with an eye turned my way. All the shopkeepers had warned me that this Conrock was a nasty fellow. I wasn't certain if he was watching me or her, and I didn't care. Despite feeling as nervous as a C. O. on his first deployment, I decided not to let this vision of beauty disappear into the crowds.

"Excuse me, Miss," I said with the breathlessness of trying to talk while lost in a dream, "can I help you? You look lost."

When she turned those starry eyes toward me, it was like most of my brain stopped working.

"Do you..." she seemed have trouble forming her words, and spoke in a stumbling manner,

"...understand... what happiness is?"

"What makes you think I would know that?" It was a crazy question to ask a stranger.

"Your smile." She gently caressed the edges of my lips with her fingertips. Her touch was electric.

"You know, I think I'm starting to. I'd like to help you find it, too."

I wasn't lying, because I can't ever remember feeling like I did when she took my hand and walked with me. What followed felt like a fairy tale, even though communication was difficult since she seemed new to the English language. I treated her to a fine dinner and was not surprised to discover that she was a vegan—not from the Vega system, but an eater of plants. I then took her to the festival activities on the upper levels, where we shook loose our shadow, Conrock.

I felt proud when the fear in her eyes dimmed and was replaced by another look as we danced to the music of the elites on gossamer webs in open air. I have to admit that I started to laugh when my former employer saw us and his jaw fell slack. When he moved in the direction of the ushers, I decided it was time to leave, and we headed back to the ground and a snug little ale shop that was on my protection list.

My little beauty claimed to have no name, but when she started to smile, I was too distracted to think about how strange that was.

"So this is happy?"

I pulled her closer to me, and she did not shrink when I leaned in for a long kiss. Her physical response was crystal clear, even as my mind muddled.

I apologized for the lack of proper lighting when we reached my apartment.

"You do not need to see love," she murmured sweetly as she again touched my lips, "to know that it is there."

Perhaps we both overreacted to feelings of joy and interpreted them into stronger emotion, but she stirred a fire in me that I had never felt before. She tenderly peeled free her only garment, and her skin seemed to glow in the dark. There was an aurora around her like that of an angel.

That night I forgot how I was a lonely stray adrift amongst the flotsam of the stars, a refugee from my own past with no light to guide me. She inspired me to remember my passion for the stars.

It was much later before we lay exhausted on my rickety bed. She was so damn beautiful and innocent as she slept, a soft hum in her throat as I stroked her incomparable wings that I never wanted to let her go. But the readiness of our union plagued me. I wanted to stay right there with her, but with as swiftly as we had bonded, I was certain that I would never see her again after this night. So I decided to give her something to remember me by.

Like a ghost I slipped from bed, dressed and gathered every credit that I had, and wrote a note promising my quick return, wondering the whole time if she would even be able to read it. As I slipped quietly out the door, I immediately felt pangs of anxiety, worried that she might not be there when I returned.

Pounding on a shop door, I used foul words to rouse the owner with warnings that I might forget to watch for his safety. Standing there idly with time to think, an instinct began to prickle at the back of my brain as the shopkeeper mumbled and grumbled on the other side of the door, repeating my words in a fashion that he thought I might not understand. By the time he finally opened, I had already disappeared down the dusky street, my gut sending me home in a sprint.

It seemed that whenever I am about to encounter something bad, my back muscles contort and feel like a demon is breathing on them. That feeling was palpable when I reached my apartment and saw the flames leaping from the window.

When I burst into the smoke-filled room, it was strewn with bloodstained wreckage. My vision of perfection was stretched across the floor, her lovely wings brutally amputated, and her skin scraped raw to remove all the gems from her pores.

I carried her surprisingly light body out into the fresh air and cradled her in my arms, watching as her eyes turned milky, and cried for the first time since I was a child.

"Life is short," she choked. "Thank you... for

keeping mine from being... wasted."

She stiffened in a moment of panic that faded rapidly as all the light left her eyes, and she went limp. All the ambitions that she had awakened in me died with her, but at the same time I came to a realization. She had taught me to live for today, and I began to recognize all the errors I had made in life.

I reluctantly delivered her body to the District infirmary. Although I would have preferred to tend to her services myself, there were things that I had to do. Revenge is a powerful motivator.

I was not surprised when Conrock arrived at the infirmary, shaking his head when he saw her on the cart.

"I was afraid of this."

"Afraid of what?" I demanded. "Who did this?"

Conrock patted her head.

"I would have warned you earlier, but I didn't want to spook you," he replied. "I saw how you two were responding to each other, and tried to run interference, but some city official you'd pissed off wanted you arrested. That was when I lost you in the maze."

"Warned me about what?"

"She comes from the planet Phileas, which has shunned outworlder colonization. People say it's another Wild Stars world, like Magnus IV. Ever since the Unification Government came to power, they've been open to exploitation by the Reavers from the Black Star system."

"What kind of exploitation are you talking about?"

"Silicatein."

"Huh...?"

"Phileans secrete Silicatein. It's a protein that is nearly impossible to reproduce, because it's a unique hybrid of minerals and proteins in a crystalline assembly."

"I thought those jewels on her skin looked real."

"They were... and are incredibly valuable. Other parts of their bodies are considered to be aphrodisiacs, while their wings are high fashion. Since the Black Star system joined the Artomique's Unification Government while Phileas is an independent Wild Stars world, the Reavers are free to hunt the Phileans at will."

"That's an atrocity!"

"That's the boundaries of decision. She must have had quite a run of kindness from strangers to make it this far, but I saw four Reavers follow her down from the spaceport. There was nothing I could do until they broke Trovadorian law. I was hoping *you* might run some interference."

I was stupefied and outraged to learn that a government I had served was indirectly responsible for my angel being brutally butchered. I sank to my knees, still clutching to the edge of the cadaver cart while Conrock explained that the Reavers had not broken any laws. It took me a moment to understand why he continued talking.

"Those Reavers are no better than beasts," said Conrock. "They wear metal atmospheric converters in their necks, which in some markets is valued as highly as Philean hides. It easy to spot them from distance, even though they tend to frequent the shadows. They're probably back in the alleys of my District, right now."

He said no more after I saw the glint of steel in his eyes, and I nodded. Even though he certainly saw that I was filled with a rage that bordered on insanity, he looked the other way when I left the infirmary.

It did not take long to locate the Reavers, then harass them and let them think that they had me cornered in that dead-end alley. They were armed, and I wasn't. But I didn't need a weapon, and used every hand-to-hand killing technique that I'd ever learned in the military.

A lucky shot from the last Reaver that got me as I ripped out his throat apparatus. It was an ugly death, one so gruesome and grisly that I would have never thought that I'd be capable of inflicting it. But I'd never been hurt so deeply before, and enjoyed it.

All that's left for me to do now is to find a way to Phileas, the home of my perfect angel. I think I could find more happiness there than I ever could on a supposedly civilized world. Maybe I can even do something to stop the Reavers. Maybe the throat apparatuses will be worth enough to get me offworld, and I can return to her family the remains I recovered.

Still, something is wrong.

Everything is so dark and remote. It's like I'm stuck in a dream. I recall an old acquaintance approaching me even as I contemplated my next steps. Yes. It was Jeanne Filaire from the Institute. What could she be doing on Trovador? She was whisked away to the fine life by a representative of the government I've learned to hate. I hope she hasn't suffered a fate similar to mine!

I guess I need to accept that life does not always hold the answers you're hoping for. I'll concede to the darkness and won't cower from it. If I have died, then I'm ready, even thought there are so many things that I now wish I could do differently.

Hope is but a sigh.

Chapter Three
When All is Said and Done

Jeanne Filaire felt a tear rolling down her cheek as Conrock removed the interrogation device from James Forester's head. The breath of the prone man surged for a moment, and then fell into the normal cadence of deep sleep.

"What are you going to do?" Jeanne asked Conrock.

"The law is clear. He'll be punished as befits his crimes. I may not have liked the Reavers, but they were citizens of the Unification Government."

"But you're the one who sent him after them!"

"You'd best forget that little detail," he replied with a stern tone of voice that frightened Jeanne and made her take a step backwards.

Conrock methodically reached for his transmitter.

"Please, don't!" she pleaded as her tears became a torrent.

Conrock seemed suddenly confused at the sight of her crying.

"There are only animals here on the ground level," Jeanne continued, "and you know James doesn't deserve to be locked up in a jail with them."

"The law prescribes liquidation."

Jeanne felt as though she had been slapped.

"You know what?" She declared, "I'm proud that he did what he did. I remember feathers like those he mentioned from my past, when I was a plaything for the rich. I never asked where they, or the jewelry, or any of the other gifts came from. Knowing what I know now, I'm glad that they rejected me and took it all away--glad that they're all gone from my life. If I'd known the truth of things then, I would have made different choices."

"Now you sound like him, spouting about how you understood what the truth of life is. So tell me, how else are you going to learn what the truth is, if you don't live it? Life is making corrections as you grow."

Conrock paused, waiting for an answer, but Jeanne only offered him ashamed silence. Conrock adjusted his shoulders and cleared his throat.

"Jeanne," he said, "I know you hate living in Trovador. Everyone on the ground does. What would you say if I offered you a way out?"

"No, thank you," she replied as politely as she could, having heard many such false offers in the past. She knew the routine and how no one ever lived up to their end of a bargain after they had gotten what they wanted. Her only hope was to find someone powerful enough that they might be able to deliver on their promise. Then it would be up to her to persuade them to follow through.

"You like it here... with the animals?"

"I'll find my own way out. Listen to me, Conrock. About James ..."

"Forget James. I'm talking about you. What options could you possibly have to get you out of here?" The authority in Conrock's voice battered her like a ram. "My God, Jeanne. That's the same thing you just escaped from. Don't tell me, you've taken someone's offer?"

Jeanne nodded.

"You're going to end up just like that poor 'angel.'"

Jeanne shrugged and turned away.

"I really have nothing left to lose."

"Jeanne..." Conrock muttered.

At first she ignored him, but when she cast a backward look she realized that he had drawn his weapon and aimed it at her.

"That's prostitution, Jeanne. That's a crime."

The stun blast caught her full between the eyes.

Conrock grabbed her before she hit the ground, and laid her on the couch next to Forester. He then called Central Control.

"This is Conrock. Has the street crew finished cleaning up? Good. So have I, my interrogation is concluded. Remember that clause I discussed in the Unification sanctions? Yeah. I've got two undesirables here who, without a doubt will never step back into Unification territory once they're out. So, by Section Eight, Article Two, we can ferry them to the starport under custody and ship them wherever we choose outside legal territories, thus liquidating the presence of undesirables by means other than termination. Right? Right! Send a pickup up to my frequency, I'll leave the transmitter on. And... thanks!"

Conrock took a moment to smile. He had felt too long like Sisyphus trying to forever push a boulder up a mountain. Looking at the blissfully sleeping couple he began to muse aloud.

"That 'angel' said she didn't want her life to be wasted. You gave her a moment of happiness, and now I've giving you both a chance at that gift. That's how I get mine."

Heroes & Villains of the Wild Stars

Achilles Hister [The Elder]

Class/Type: Fighting Man / Mastermind / Tech Specialist

Approximate Level: Mid-to-High-Level

Skills & Background: Though capable of defending himself and crushing his enemies, Achilles Hister's greatest weapons are his mind and his patience. The head of the Artomiques has access to impressive

stolen Wild Stars technology that was light-years beyond what 20th Century Earth was capable of producing; much of this stolen technology was used to bring Earth 'up to speed' over the course of two centuries with the Artomiques in a position to be the dominant political force on Earth. How over two centuries? Stolen Wild Stars cloning and mind-transference technology, of course!

Achilles Hister is the son of Adolf Hister, a parallel universe version of our world's Adolf Hitler. When time travelling Wild Stars stopped the Artomique conquest of earth in their universe, the timeline in which the fascists won World War II collapsed. Achilles Hister and a few loyal henchmen escaped into our timeline, first attempting to recreate their old timeline, later making the best of things using the stolen Wild Star technology to implement the Artomique Paradigm in this world.

Ancient Warrior

Class/Type: Fighting Man

Approximate Level: High-Level/Demigod

Skills & Background: The Ancient Warrior is a master swordsman and martial artist. His weapons of choice include single-handed swords and "sticks" [two-piece staves]. He is also a more-than-capable pilot of single-person watercraft, a skill which also translates to space craft.

The Ancient Warrior is a member of an immortal race of humanoid aliens but he was adopted and raised by mortals. Immortality is a burden and madness must be kept carefully at bay; so much time has passed since his youth that he has forgotten much of his past and who he was.

The Ancient Warrior notably led mankind on its exodus to the stars when Atlantis fell, in many ways becoming a father-figure to the Wild Stars, however he eschews any notions of godhood that other megalomaniacal immortals that escaped to our universe entertain.

His greatest motivation is to be reunited with his childhood love, Phaedra, another immortal who has, over the aeons, forgotten him.

Bullson

Class/Type: Fighting Man / Psionicist

Approximate Level: Mid-Level

Skills & Background: Bullson is an incredibly talented fighter, especially with a sword. His real weapon though is his Time Travel Device that allows for him to

have lightning-quick reflexes in a fight as well as jump through time and space at his convenience. His mother also taught him telepathy which, when used in conjunction with his fighting skills and time travel device, which makes him nearly unbeatable in combat.

Bullson is the result of an illicit (and not entirely willing/knowing) union between Bully Bravo and the God Mother, one of the immortal aliens vying for power in the cosmic struggle against her fellow immortals. He was "created" for the purpose of assisting the Ancient Warrior rescue Phaedra. As a pawn, though an incredibly powerful one, Bullson struggles to find an identity and a cause that is truly his own.

Bully Bravo
Class/Type: Fighting Man / Professional Adventurer / Negotiator
Approximate Level: Mid-Level
Skills & Background: Bully Bravo is a renowned Jack-of-all-Trades. A skilled leader and negotiator, Bully is often sent in to assess and deal with unknown situations and to make first contact. His Wild Stars universal translator combined with his political acumen and 'plain-folk wisdom' makes him a valuable asset in any circumstance. He's also a capable fighter in a scrap, and good with a gun, for the few situations he can't talk his way out of.

Bully Bravo is something of a champion of the everyman, and most folks who meet him recognize this right away. This helped him win a term as President of Earth and be seen as a major force of influence when the Wild Stars, Earth, and her Colony Worlds came together for the first time in official political contact with one another. He's honest and trustworthy—rare traits in a politician—and will often throw in with the underdog against the corrupt and oppressors.

Daestar
Class/Type: Psionicist / Spy
Approximate Level: Mid-to-High-Level
Skills & Background: Though slight and not a physical fighter by any means, Daestar is a powerful telepath whose empathic skills and cunning have gotten her through several tight scrapes.

Daestar is a member of the mysterious telepaths guild, the Five-Thousand Fingered Hand, originally tasked to create a Book of Circles—a psychic recording of memories and events—around the Ancient Warrior and his family in the Wild Stars. On her mission, she fell in love Erlik, the Ancient Warrior's immortal son. Despite her connections to the Hand, Daestar is devoted to both her husband and her father-in-law. She will often be found in the company of Erlik and would do anything for him or her family. Other telepaths may consider her a renegade for turning her back on the Hand.

Dalucar Zonderman
Class/Type: Specialist | Technician | AI
Approximate Level: High-Level/Demigod
Skills & Background: Dalucar is the last known

surviving Saturnian, though at present, he exists only as an advanced string of AI code that allows him to take over any computerized device with external access.

The Eybontic-Saturnian War was one of the greatest travesties wrought by the Artomique's theft of Wild Star technology. The Saturnian cyborgs possessed highly advanced quantum neural processors and their consciousness could be transferred to new clone bodies regularly. They eventually defeated the Eybontics, humanoid robots originally used for deep space exploration, but at great cost to both factions. While the Eybontics were mostly destroyed, the remaining Saturnians ultimately cannibalized each other for parts until only Dalucar remained.

Erlik

Class/Type: Fighting Man
Approximate Level: High-Level
Skills & Background: Erlik is one of the

strongest warriors and best swordsmen among the Wild Stars. He also possesses a Time Travel Device, which allowed him once to search for his kidnapped grand-daughter across a billion years in a single day.

Erlik is the son of the Ancient Warrior and one of the foremost princes of the Wild Stars. His mother was a telepathic assassin who betrayed the Ancient Warrior. Like his father, he is an immortal. Despite this, Erlik is level-headed and grounded [thanks in part to his beloved wife Daestar]. He is a champion of justice and he hates traitors and cowards. He is also devoted to his friends and family and would lay down his life for them.

Genghis Champlain

Class/Type: Fighting Man / Martial Artist
Approximate Level: Mid-to-High-Level
Skills & Background: From firearms to close

combat weapons to hand-to-hand, Genghis has trained in all of the martial arts, and over the course of his unnaturally extended lifetime, has not only mastered them but honed them to perfection, making him one of the most deadly weapons in the Artomiques arsenal.

Before the destruction of original Artomique timeline, Genghis was a Field Marshal of the Artomique army. He is absolutely devoted to Achilles Hister and the Artomiques' cause, however he would prefer a restoration of the Artomique timeline to an Artomique domination over this one.

Georgian Raveling

Class/Type: Fighting Man / Agent
Approximate Level: Mid-to-High-Level

Skills & Background: Georgian is a tough-as-nails soldier skilled in both combat and tracking. With an artificially extended lifespan, Georgian has had several lifetimes to polish his skills.

Georgian was First Specialist Officer in the Artomique Army, part of their air cavalry. Like Genghis, Georgian continues to serve directly under Achilles Hister in this timeline and acts as his chief special ops agent.

Montchuhasus
Class/Type: Fighting Man / Navigator
Approximate Level: Mid-Level
Skills & Background: While a capable swordsman and one of the wielders of the legendary Toridian blades, Montchuhasus true talent is that of a pilot and a navigator. He is the last of Mu, and can "read" magnetic lines to chart his courses.

As an ancient Atlantean sailor, Montchuhasus is truly a man out of time and out of place. Like all ancient sea-farers, Montchuhasus is fearless in the face of the unknown beyond the horizon. He was the right man who was where he needed to be when he needed to be for the Ancient Warrior, else he might have joined the rest of mankind on their original journey to the stars. His skill in piloting boats was so great that the Ancient Warrior recruited him to navigate a space ship through a black hole, which he did successfully to aid in rescuing Phaedra from the God Father.

Red Queen
Class/Type: Psionicist / Rogue
Approximate Level: High-Level
Skills & Background:
The Red Queen is not only a charming and devious space pirate, she is also one of the few known telepaths more powerful than Daestar. One of her most devastating attacks is her Psychic Knife which can completely disable a rival telepath. Whether by her charms, cunning, or

psychic powers, the Red Queen can get just about anything she wants with relative ease.

The Red Queen is actually one of a set of twins; sometimes Nefarimor, sometimes ice cream heiress "Scarlet Tanager," the Red Queen is the notorious leader of a band of space pirates based on Corsairiana, a planet fitted with engines to turn it into a giant spaceship. The death of her twin sister may have thrown a wrench in her plans, but an alliance with Achilles Hister and the Artomique Corporation makes her one of the two most dangerous figures in the galaxy. She also has connections with the Five-Thousand Fingered Hand.

Whip, Achilles Hister [The Younger]
Class/Type: Fighting Man / Tech Specialist
Approximate Level: Low-Level
Skills & Background: Whip is a sharp young man with his father's keen and intelligent mind (somewhat literally). He has an aptitude for technology. Georgian and Genghis have acted as his

guardians and mentors, though really they are just keeping tabs on him for his father. While he has picked up some training from the two of them, he has not had the experience to make much practical use of it yet.

Achilles Hister Senior has actually been using stolen Wild Stars technology to create a succession of clones and, using mind transference, achieve a sort of immortality—Whip is just his latest clone. While Whip sees himself as his father's son, and while he respects him, he wants to walk his own path and take the Artomique Corporation in a different direction. Unfortunately, his father only sees him as the next "body" to use.